Trusting Claire

ALYSSA HALL

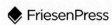 FriesenPress

Suite 300 - 990 Fort St
Victoria, BC, V8V 3K2
Canada

www.friesenpress.com

This book may be purchased in bulk for promotional, educational or business use. For information about bulk discounts, please contact Alyssa Hall at www.alyhallwriter.com

ISBN
978-1-5255-9070-2 (Hardcover)
978-1-5255-9069-6 (Paperback)
978-1-5255-9071-9 (eBook)

1. FICTION, THRILLERS, CRIME

Distributed to the trade by The Ingram Book Company

Printed in Canada

Don't trust everything you see.
Even salt can look like sugar.

List of Characters
In Order of Appearance

Spring 1987, in a town outside Toronto

Chapter 1

"Are you still awake?" asked the voice when she picked up the phone.

"Just getting ready for bed," she replied. "What's wrong, Will?"

"Would you please come over? Right now?" he asked. She let out a sigh and, with feigned protest, she responded.

"Will, it's almost 9:00. It's getting dark!"

The pause on the end of the line conveyed his disappointment. Endeavouring to tempt her further, he continued, "You don't want to miss this, Claire. It's beautiful up here! The moon is out, there's a breeze, and it's moving these incredible scents around in the air. Somewhere I thought I heard an owl. Also, the crickets are chirping, and it's warm as hell. It's the perfect night for you to come. But I called because the horses are out. I know you want to see the horses."

She really did want to see him and, to be honest, the idea of going at this time sounded like the best thing for her to do. It had been a hectic day, and she liked—no, *loved*—the spontaneity of it. Telling him she'd be there in half an hour, she scrambled into her sweats and t-shirt, then ran to the mirror to tie her hair back and do a quick face check. Tiptoeing across the hall to her roommate's door, she tapped to see if she was still awake.

"Who was that on the phone?" Kate asked.

"It was Will," Claire answered as she walked into the room. "I'm going over there now. He says the horses are out." Even as she uttered the words, she knew what was coming.

Kate gave her a look that was becoming all too familiar these days and said, "Are you serious, Claire? What if Ben calls?"

Claire turned and walked towards the door, dismissively waving her hand in the air. "Tell him I'm sleeping", she answered.

"I hope you know what you are doing," Kate said before she gently closed the door again.

Claire had first met Kate back in high school, when she had been a classmate of Claire's younger brother, Paul. Back in those days, she and Kate paid little attention to one another, being five grades apart and in different crowds. Years later, after becoming re-acquainted at Paul's wedding, they fell into a quasi-friendship. They realized how well they got on together when by chance both went to work for the same real estate company. Claire worked as the listing photographer and Kate closing deals. Then, when an opportunity materialized to share a home, they both jumped at the chance.

Despite the age difference, they had progressed from roommates to confidants, advisors, and friends. Kate had recently divorced from what had become a bad situation, and her mother often reminded her that she had married too young. Having come away jaded, she could no longer understand why anyone would want to bother with relationships. Claire, on the other hand, had a very rose-colored attitude towards all matters concerning the heart. She also knew that the likelihood of Ben calling was slim, and that Kate was simply making a point.

She ran down the stairs pausing on the landing to grab her keys and walked out into the warm night. She turned to lock the door and climbed into her car. Backing out of the driveway, Claire thought about what Kate had said. She and Ben had been casually acquainted for nearly six months, now. Although Ben made it obvious that he would love more of a commitment from her, he was careful not to push her. Claire really cared for him, but she just wasn't ready for anything more.

But thinking about Ben wasn't what she wanted to be doing at this moment. She was annoyed that Kate had to mention him just as she was walking out the door. She and Ben were little more than friends at this point, so she felt no strong loyalty to him. It was no secret that Kate disapproved of Will. She called him pretentious, among other things. Driving out to see him, Claire felt innocent enough, but now in a somewhat dishonest way.

Claire had met Will at a social function, only a short while ago. That evening, he was a breath of fresh air, distracting her from her life. He was a big man, and he wore his self-assuredness with a casual coolness, and she instantly fell under his spell. Her time with him slowed things down, as if hours didn't exist. She found his presence calming, and she liked the fact that he had no expectations.

As she exited from the main road, she realized that Will had not been wrong—it really was a beautiful evening. She could still see the watercolor pink of the sun on the horizon. There was a rosy glow of light ahead of her, enticing her forward. There was total darkness behind her. She thought it was a beautiful metaphor, her driving to Will - the light that lay ahead. She felt her foot put extra pressure to the gas pedal.

Suddenly, Claire couldn't wait to be with him.

Claire had grown up with an immense love of music. Music had enlivened her during her somewhat insular childhood. This had started with listening to her grandfather playing his Russian records. Her favourite was a song called Mama, by Lubomyr Maciuk. This was long before she grew to love modern music. Her imagination grew through music, and she had developed this funny little fantasy where, from time to time, she was providing the soundtrack to her life as Clara Perova, Musical Director Extraordinaire. She turned up the radio to the new song by INXS, "I Need You Tonight." She could not have picked a more fitting song.

Chapter 2

Claire met Will three months ago, when she and Kate were attending the semi-annual Town Centre dance. These dances were extremely popular in the community. They were a good opportunity for local bands to show off their talents, and they also provided a venue for everyone to catch up with neglected friends. This was a good way to compensate for busy lives. Women could show off new hairdos, their outfits, and the latest photographs of their children, while guys could talk about cars, sports, and music, or just girl watch. It was unusual for Claire to attend these dances unless she was looking for referrals for her work, but tonight Kate had been reluctant to attend on her own. So, on this particular evening, having no real business opportunities, she found herself in a less than pleasant situation.

Looking around the room, Claire absorbed her surroundings. Never being much of a fashion aficionado, she admired the effort that women put into their wardrobes, with their shoulder-padded blouses and parachute pants. Big-headed perms were in abundance, the bigger the better. People on the dance floor were giving their best impressions of the Roger Rabbit to the tune of "I Love Rock and Roll," while a few of the men, clad in their high-top sneakers went so far as to attempt the Moonwalk.

After an hour or so, Claire was more than ready to leave. How would she manage to stick it out for the rest of the evening? This was more Kate's thing, being younger and having more connection to these people. Having said that, Claire was quite impressed with the band. The musicians were very good, and it was definitely a step up from the usual rock and roll music that bar bands tended to play. Currently, an excellent version of "Lovers In a Dangerous Time" by Bruce Cockburn was being played, which was not an easy song to tackle. "Good for them," she thought to herself. But once she had made the rounds saying 'hello' to everyone and having had a glass of wine, Claire was done. She began searching the crowd for a glimpse of Kate to let her know that she was leaving.

It was at that moment that Will walked into the room. Claire knew who he was, but they had never spoken more than a few words to each other. Will had been her neighbour growing up. He had lived a few miles down her street—past her house, but still technically a neighbour. She would sometimes see his car go by, since the only way to the main road was past her house. Will now ran a small car repair shop on the edge of town.

The doorway was across the room, but their eyes met as soon as he came in. Claire felt her breath quicken. Serendipity. Unlike the well-groomed Ben, Will had a ruggedness about him, with dark shaggy hair coming just below his shirt collar and the smallest hint of a beard. It was hard not to spot him in a crowd, given his 6'3" frame. Keeping his eyes on her, he made his way over to where she was standing.

She felt a little self-conscious because of the way he had singled her out.

All he said was, "Claire, right?" with a big grin.

"Hi Will," she replied. "Wow, it's great to see you here. And I'm actually quite surprised, I have never seen you at one of these events."

He replied with a laugh, "Aha, how could you possibly know me so well? I was dragged here by my buddy Glen," he continued. "He thought it would do me good to get out," at which point he stepped slightly to one side to acknowledge Glen. Standing behind him, his small frame was shadowed by Will's. "Claire, Glen. Glen, Claire." Without making eye contact, Glen mumbled a hello before disappearing into the crowd.

She blurted out, "I have to be honest, I'm really happy that Glen succeeded." She felt a bit too cheerful but somehow, she couldn't help herself.

Will looked down at her and said, "Come on, blue eyes, let me get us a drink."

Claire looked around and asked, "But what about Glen? Where did he go?"

Will smiled, and his eyes wrinkled up. "Don't worry about him, he's right at home at these shindigs."

He took her by the arm and gently steered her towards the bar.

Sitting away from the band in a quiet area of the hall, they easily fell into conversation. Will's eyes hardly left hers as he leaned forward, elbows on knees. Will talked about how he loved his quiet life in his small cottage on the outskirts of town. He spoke with energy, and his descriptions were vivid. Maybe Claire was attracted to Will because he represented the opposite of everything she knew and was. Perhaps he was the bad boy that kept her on the edge and messed with her sensibilities. That evening, while trying hard not to think of Ben, she had renewed misgivings about what she wanted. She had arrived with Kate but that night, Will drove her home.

Will spoke of his love of the outdoors. How he preferred to spend every waking minute outside and simply loved being lost in nature. Claire felt drawn to him in an inexplicable way. She enjoyed his descriptions of kayak trips to Orr Lake in the spring, when the loons were mating. She was charmed when he said that he loved the sound of the pouring rain, sometimes going outside just to stand in it. Will was definitely born for the country.

She, on the other hand, loved living in town, loved the excitement of her career and having people around her. For all of the negative aspects attached to noisy, busy urban areas, she preferred them to isolation. Still, she loved Will's passion for his life. She began spending time with him almost immediately after that night. Despite their differences—or perhaps because of them—their rendezvous did her a world of good. The encounters began as intimate dinners or a movie. More recently, they'd been having more visits like this one—the kind that took them straight to his bedroom, where they remained until morning.

Before she realized it, Claire arrived at the lane that led to his cottage. As she pulled off the road, she could make out his distinguishable silhouette by the gate, waiting for her to arrive.

"Hi Cee," he whispered to her as he opened her door. "I am happy that you came out. Thank you." Without another word, he gave her hand a quick squeeze and led her to an area by the pond that was encased in moonlight. He pointed to the right, where she could now see the horses and hear them gently snorting.

Will explained that he stopped to see them every evening when he returned from work. Before long, they began waiting for him by the fence, and they would run to the fence and neigh excitedly at the sound of his tires on the gravel. One of the horses walked over to Claire, and she leaned over to stroke its muzzle. She had the impression that this one was a white Andalusian breed, and that it was very well cared for. Will put an arm around her and cooed gently to the magnificent beasts.

He placed some apple in her hand, and she reached over the fence to feed them. Of all her visits, this was the first time that the horses had come to the fence to say hello. She was grateful for this. She looked up at Will, his face bathed in the soft light of the moon. She sensed that she would never forget this moment. The evening had a whimsical feel to it that perfectly captured the moonlight, the horses, the pond, and Will.

Chapter 3

Two days later, Will called her. It seemed really late, maybe because she had gone to bed early. Roused from her slumber, she picked up the phone. He whispered her name and then abruptly hung up. She held the phone in her hand for a few minutes and waited for him to call back. But soon, she leaned over and put it back in its cradle. She tried to stay awake, but sleep overcame her. By morning, she had forgotten about it.

Late that afternoon, just as Claire was getting ready to leave her office, she received a call from Kate. It had been a busy day, and Claire was eager to get out of the office. She debated not answering, but she changing her mind and reached for the phone. The message was short and concise. Will was dead. Apparently, he was found face down in a pond beside his cottage, and it wasn't yet known how long he had been there before being discovered..

"I called as soon as I heard the news," Kate said, some concern in her voice. "They have not given any more information at this point, only that they plan on investigating whether the death was accidental. They have not ruled out foul play. Do you think they might want to talk to you, Claire?"

Overwhelmed with mixed emotions, Claire struggled to understand what she had just heard. Could this really be happening? She tried to pack up her things, but sat there, paralyzed. Her head was spinning so that standing up right now was not an option.

"What the Hell is going on?" she muttered to herself. Gathering her composure she left the office, still in a daze. Everything looked different as she was driving along the same streets she took every day. The buildings looked worn and tired. She noticed the dipped and pot-holed roads as if she was seeing them for the first time. The sky looked grey, her hands on the steering wheel looked old. It was an anguish that she hadn't experienced for a very long time.

There was a place where she had often met Will, just a short distance from her house. Rather than go straight home, Claire drove to that spot, to sit for a moment and gather her thoughts. She got out of her car and headed towards a bench that overlooked a park. The grass beneath her feet was crisp and fragrant from a recent cutting. Sitting down, she glanced at the sentiments that were carved into the wood: "David loves Sara forever." The dark clouds moved quickly across an angry sky while the wind coaxed the trees into a chaotic dance. Claire breathed in the life around her. From where she sat, she could see groups of older teens playing baseball. She never could understand the excitement over a game where everyone seemed to be standing around.

Her mind took her back to a particular rainy day she had spent with Will, shortly after she met him. Will had driven them south, to a mega movie theatre that was showing a re-run of Blade Runner. For some reason this particular day was deeply ingrained in her memory. They shared popcorn and softly whispered to each other, each recalling their favourite parts of the film. They were still there long after the credits were finished, neither of them in a hurry to leave.

Only a few days later, he called her to meet him at Mill Pond, near the village of Kettleby. He had packed hot dogs and white wine, and they had an impromptu picnic. Hopping into his car, they drove on to the general store to buy water and candy. They climbed the two steps onto the creaky wooden porch and entered the dusty old building, the wooden screen door slamming behind them. The shelves were packed with dry goods, and on the counter there were big glass jars of penny candy. Giggling like school kids they stuffed their mouths full of black licorice and drank it down with cold water. All of their encounters had revolved around the two of them being alone, Will having created opportunities for them to get to know one another. It seemed very romantic to her, the way he took care to plan them. And now, just like that, he was gone.

The next few days felt almost like a dream. Claire had the sensation that she was looking down on herself, existing but not feeling, just going through the motions. This was having an unsettling impact on her. The thought of death—that it could be so sudden—sent a chill through her body. She had not experienced the death of someone close to her since her grandparents died, so these emotions were still new to her.

The following evening, as she and Kate were sharing a meal together in reflective quietude, there was a knock at the door and two police officers stood on the doorstep. One officer stepped forward to address her.

"Are you Claire Perova? I'm Officer Cooper, and this is my

partner, Officer Smitty. I hope this is not an inconvenient time for you, but may we please come in? We need to ask you a few questions about Will Elliott's death."

"Yes," she stammered. "Please come in." She invited them into the front room, where Kate had emerged to see who was at the door. On Claire's insistence, Kate stayed in the room with her as she suddenly felt nervous, almost sick to her stomach. She motioned the officers to sit in the two easy chairs. She and Kate sat on the sofa opposite. They were respectfully subdued; she was sure this was required protocol when investigating a death. They were both hefty men, and they filled the room. One was much older than the other and looked more military, with short hair and sharp green eyes. He sported a tattoo on the back of his wrist.

As the questioning began, Claire realized that she didn't have much information to give them. She had only known Will for a few months, she didn't know any of his family or friends, and she had last seen him two days before his death. It turned out that Will, without a doubt, had been a stranger to her. This shouldn't have come as a surprise. After all, it takes months, sometimes even years to really know someone. And it would still depend on whether or not the person wanted to be known. Did Will want to be known?

The officers looked at each other in silence before the young one, Cooper, cleared his throat and readjusted his position in the chair. Although the younger of the two men, he seemed to be the senior ranking officer. Claire's thought that he wore his uniform like a peacock in heat, and his manner towards her was slightly discourteous.

"Did you know this guy at all?"

He had a sarcastic tone that she didn't appreciate, and at that moment she made up her mind that they shared a mutual hostility.

Kate looked up at Claire before offering, "She hasn't known him for very long," unsure whether this comment would help or hinder.

"So, tell me again, you said you didn't know anything about this man at all, yet there you were," choosing to ignore Kate altogether.

The older officer Smitty interjected by thanking her for speaking with them, and could she please think back and try to remember if there was anything unusual about Will's behavior the last time she saw him.

"Well, all I can think of is that he had a very bad dream the last night I was there. Oh, and a day or two after that night, he called me really late, but he hung up right away. He didn't call back." That was all she could offer. For her to say that she noticed nothing unusual about his behavior sounded idiotic. How did she know what his usual behavior would be?

"That's fine, Miss. We can stop there for now. Any bit of information might help, so please do call if you think of anything else, even if it doesn't sound important to you at the time. And you too, Miss," he said as he turned towards Kate. And with that, Smitty handed each of them his card.

"Thank you, officer, I will," Claire nodded.

The two men didn't stay long afterwards, and they soon stood to leave. Officer Smitty thanked them for their time and said that he would call again if any further clarification was needed. As the officers exited, the two women, in what could almost have been a planned agreement, deliberately said goodbye only to Smitty. Officer Cooper could go to hell.

Chapter 4

THE FOLLOWING AFTERNOON, CLAIRE LEFT THE OFFICE IN a hurry, wanting nothing more than to be at home. She still didn't feel like herself, and she needed to distance herself from the world. She let out a sigh when she pulled up to her house and saw Ben's car parked in front. She got out of her car, and he immediately walked towards her. Claire was to 5'6" to Ben's 5'10", so they almost met eye to eye. She looked at the ground and said, "I can't do this anymore."

He put his hand under her chin and lifted her face up to meet his. "What can't you do anymore?" he asked.

"This! It's no good, Ben. Something has changed. I think I need some time."

He took her hand gently. "Hey look, I know you've been having difficulty since this person's death and I wish there was something I could do that would make a difference to you. I'm feeling a bit useless here, Claire. But can we talk for a while? Let's go inside and let me pour us a glass of wine."

Claire did like Ben. He was grounding even in the midst of this disquietude. She had met him a year ago at her bank, where he worked as manager. He would come out of his glass office to greet her at the till whenever he spotted her coming in. Although she had known him for longer, the dating began shortly before she met Will. She still remembered the day he mustered up the courage to ask her to have lunch with him. Ben was a single father to a young boy, and although he and Claire saw a fair amount of each other, over-nights were off limits. Most of their time spent together was during the day in the company of his son, allowing them precious few moments for any form of intimacy. Ben believed in easing into things and had been cautious. He also seemed uncomfortable talking about his failed marriage, and it wasn't clear where the child's mother was.

Ben went to the car and grabbed her briefcase and camera bags while she unlocked the front door. He followed her through to the pale-yellow kitchen, bright with natural light. The large windows opened up to a lush backyard and small patio area, nicely decorated with pots of flowers and four blue lounging chairs. Ben went to the glass cupboard where the wine glasses were kept, while Claire retrieved the opened bottle of Chenin Blanc from the fridge. Once they settled on a pair of white kitchen stools with their wine, Ben broke the silence by saying, "Isn't there a song that says, 'It Was Good Now It's Gone'?"

Claire laughed, "I think it went, 'Didn't We Almost Have It All'. Wasn't that it?"

Ben looked at her in mock alarm and said, "No, wasn't it, 'I never loved you anyway'?"

They looked at each other for a moment without a word, a smile starting to form at the corners of her mouth.

"Okay," she finally said. "I get your point, Ben. I just feel overwhelmed by it all. I suppose it's normal for me to feel shocked. I mean—wow, the guy is *dead*! I realize it could have been a car crash, or cancer, or he could have choked on a bone, but this way just seems so creepy. What if it wasn't an accidental death?"

Ben leaned in and said, "Then don't shut me out, Claire. I won't push my way into your space, but I can help you through this. Keep sharing your thoughts with me. Let me know if you ever need anything."

Just then, they heard the front door close and in walked Kate, perfect timing to break the tension. She smiled in Ben's direction. "Hey, look what the cat dragged in! Hi, Ben."

Ben looked up at her and raised his glass. "Hi gorgeous. Nice to see you." She had come into the room buoyant, with an ear-to-ear-smile. Claire was pleased that there was no friction between these two important people in her life. Kate had always liked Ben, and she had made no secret about not liking Will.

Kate was a stunning beauty. There was no getting around that. She was leggy, a bit taller than Claire, with straight, waist-length dark hair to contrast with Claire's shoulder length sandy curls. She had an exotic look, her roots being Italian on her father's side and Spanish on her mother's. She was young and radiant. She was five years younger than Claire's 36, but in many ways she had years on her.

"It's almost 5:00, is anyone hungry?" she asked, as she placed a large bowl of olives on the counter. Ben got another glass and poured some wine for Kate, and the three of them moved to the back patio.

It was after 6:00 by the time Ben left. Claire thanked him for showing up like he did. The good it did her went beyond words. She felt she would sleep well tonight. She kissed him goodbye and followed him as he walked out to his car. He really is an elegant man, she thought to herself. Everything about him, from his manner of speaking to his chiseled physique, to the way he was always impeccably groomed. He spoke softly and had a gentle, kind laugh. Ben was bright, wealthy, and benevolent beyond words, and today she felt grateful for his friendship. She waved to him before heading to her editing room. She had a lot to catch up on, and she was eager to resume her assignment.

Claire had worked as a photographer for a large real estate firm where she and Kate had both been employed. She had since ventured out on her own as an independent agent. When she wasn't on the road taking photos of properties, she was busy editing (which often took longer than the photoshoot itself). It could be a high-pressure job, varying in extremes, as realtors usually need a quick turnaround time on the photos, with deadlines of 24 to 48 hours being common. Oddly, the sense of urgency had always been one of the things that Claire enjoyed most about her job.

She was currently working on a portfolio of stock photos, which could keep her fed between jobs. She had learned that a smart photographer always kept these on hand, since they could be used promotionally by any number of developers and sales agents. This could give her additional income over the long run, with less work. Claire was vying for a chance to work her way into the Toronto market, and she had recently splurged on a new Nikon camera that would help her to produce top material. Toronto was her goal, as a small-town real estate photographer was less likely to be able to charge as much as a real estate photographer in a big city. She was determined to stay on top of her game.

Chapter 5

CLAIRE'S TOWN WASN'T HUGE. THE POPULATION WAS ONLY about 80,000. She grew up on the east side of the downtown area, never venturing too far from her environs until after she left school. She had a younger brother, Paul, who was born nearly five years after her. After Claire was born, her parents had tried unsuccessfully for a second child. Then out of the blue her mother got pregnant at 42. Claire and Paul were not very close growing up, given the gender and age difference, but they loved each other.

Claire and Paul had a very sheltered upbringing. Claire thought it more dysfunctional than anything else. Their parents were Russian immigrants, and they were undeniably uncomfortable with the North American free way of life. They were short on trust and big on distancing, instilling the importance of being cautious in this uncertain world. They kept their children close to home and allowed them few friends. Claire and Paul endured endless lectures on the evils of mankind and how much better it had been in their home country. A few of the more antagonistic kids at school taunted her for being weird, and it was during the elementary years where she learned the cruelty of other children.

Claire looked average growing up, but people often told her that there was a classy attractiveness about her. Paul would say that although she was kind and considerate, she was a bit naïve and too much of a people-pleaser. Unlike Paul, she was not a socially active student who joined athletic clubs or played sports, preferring instead the quietude of the school's photography studio. Her graduation consisted of getting drunk with the other members of the photography club rather than attend prom. Mostly, she loved to spend time with her grandparents, who had immigrated with her parents. Claire was aware that she was a bit of a loner, but at this point in her life she felt no desire to be more outgoing. Being the older sibling, her parent's words may have had more impact on her, and she found that she didn't have a lot of enthusiasm for people outside her own family.

Life remained this way until after she graduated. She found that venturing out into life was a bit overwhelming, but with the help of her little brother, she discovered there was a whole world out there to explore after she completed her studies. Claire's and Paul's real friendship began in adulthood, and it was then that Claire began to sparkle.

When Claire was 23, she was in her second-year of university, working towards her BA in photography. She found that the technical experience she was receiving towards this degree was very worthwhile. She was learning about so many different types of lighting and shooting styles. Having this professional guidance was invaluable, giving prospects and a versatility that she didn't know was possible. Would she ever be able to use all of these skills? She felt eagerly optimistic about exploring the possibilities.

It was there that she met the fascinating Oliver Fisher, a fellow student with big aspirations. Oliver was a third-year student who excelled in the charisma department. It wasn't long before they fell in love and, shortly thereafter, they embarked on an educational expedition to Greece. This had long been his dream, as the Greek islands offered some amazing scenery that he had long wanted to explore, like the little churches on seawalls, ruins like the Acropolis, the white-washed buildings of Santorini. Claire had witnessed how he hard he had worked to obtain his grant to study cultural, historical and political issues. She and Oliver often spoke of this trip, and of how he planned to include his own photography with his publishing, which was his sideline. Together with Claire he hoped it could be a very productive and fulfilling trip as he felt her photographic abilities were nothing short of brilliant. It didn't take Oliver long to persuade Claire to go with him, and their plan was to stay for six months.

Saying goodbye to her family was challenging and frightening, as she had never been away from them. Paul was only eighteen, and he seemed to be in a state of shock, wondering what he would do now that his sister was abandoning him. Her grandparents looked worried, and her grandmother stood there wringing her hands in her apron.

"Why are you going?" she lamented. *pochemu ty ukhodish?*

Her parents, on the other hand, seemed to take the news very well. Maybe they thought that the experience would be good for her. Claire shared a small apartment with two other girls on the university campus, and as she packed up her belongings she bid them adieu, promising to stay in touch. She knew that six months would go by quickly, so she didn't dwell on goodbyes.

Claire and Oliver settled in Crete, in a quaint apartment overlooking Souda Bay that offered them a splendid view of the ocean and the famous lighthouse. They lived there and travelled the islands for what, quite by accident, ended up being a four-year experience. They found it impossible to leave this place, having found their essence there. Writing home, Claire explained that she decided to forego her studies in exchange for Oliver and their life in Greece. To this day, the memories fully consumed her—Georges Moustaki, endless sunsets, bouzouki music, and the distant sound of the waves caressing her to sleep each night while wrapped in Oliver's tanned, muscular arms.

But life wasn't all Tsantali and gyros—Claire had also taken a part time job working at a little restaurant in the village of Hora Sfakion. Sfakia, as it was termed by the locals, is a small coastal village located in the mountainous region on the South Coast of Crete. It was an hour's drive from where they lived, but she didn't mind the distance. It gave her the opportunity to mix with the locals while Oliver was away on one of his many research excursions. Under the tutelage of Yanni the chef, she learned to cook like a Greek, peeling the tentacle skin from octopus to make calamari and dissecting chickens in true Greek fashion. She would then try to impress Oliver with her newfound culinary skills, the delicious smells of grilled fish, lemons, and olive oil wafting through their small upper-level apartment. Her life on the island with Oliver was sheer bliss.

The people of Greece struck her as kind and gentle, always ready with a smile and a helping hand. Any passerby could enter the courtyard of a household to join a celebration in progress, be it a wedding or a birthday party. They would be welcomed like family and invited to partake in the festivities. She would always remember the two little girls who shadowed her throughout the village when she wasn't working, helpfully teaching her a plethora of Greek words that would not be in her normal day-to-day vocabulary. Claire found many similarities between Greek and Russian, so she was able to pick up quite a bit of the language.

The shepherds, whose flocks of sheep covered the hillsides, were the friendliest people to Claire. Shepherding is the oldest profession in Crete, with flocks grazing everywhere throughout the villages and in the neighbouring hills. The sound of the sheep's bells clanging around their necks became a constant, and they could be heard from most parts of the island. When the shepherds were moving the sheep through the lowlands or the town streets and they caught sight of Claire, they would smile and wave their arms.

"Kalimera Clara," they would call to her, their voices loud and friendly. They had come to know her from her hikes up the hills, practicing her Greek while snapping photos of them with their sheep. They were fascinated with the camera lens, and they were always eager to pose and strut. It was, at times, a struggle for Claire to capture them candidly, but she found their comical antics amusing.

The views from the hills left her breathless, and as she made her way back down, she found that she could unhurriedly sit for long spells. Primitive-looking shepherd's huts dotted the hillsides, visibly lending a historic feel to the area. Many of the huts contained an area inside where they made their Feta. Along with the Cretan Gruyere and the Staka, Claire felt these were the best cheeses she had ever tasted. Combined with the flavours of fresh grilled meat or fish, the island foods could easily coax one's taste buds to life.

Throughout her years in Greece, Paul wrote often, but his letters were not happy ones. Claire was gradually becoming aware that he was somehow losing his focus. The letters became listless and despondent. It seemed that after graduating, he struggled to find his footing, eventually taking on two jobs—one working mornings as a groundskeeper at a local golf course, and another at a large food store chain, where he worked evenings in the deli department, preparing the display cases with the usual variety of fare.

He wrote about the golf course, how he loved rising at dawn when the dew was still on the grass and the birds were waking up. He spent four hours every morning cutting each green in perfect diamond patterns. He would go on to explain how important it was to change the direction of the mowing pattern with each mowing, so the grass blades remained as upright as possible.

Paul's letters seemed livelier when he talked about working with food. He spoke of preferring the night job at the deli, being perpetually amazed at how much could be done with simple ingredients. She would write back saying that maybe it was their passion, as she was also immensely enjoying food preparation.

Growing up the way they did had been difficult. Neither their parents nor their grandparents spoke any English when they arrived, and comprehension was painstaking. As Paul and Claire became more aware of life through good educators, it became more and more frustrating for them, trying to explain things to the family and hitting a brick wall. One of their small comforts had been in the kitchen, watching their grandmother bake her pies and prepare various Russian dishes, such as pel'meni and knedliky, which were two versions of potato dumplings, the former stuffed, the latter not.

Exploring the Greek islands with Oliver was something Claire looked forward to, whenever she had the chance to go with him. She felt an indescribable peace wherever he took her, something almost healing. It was hard to tell if it was the people, the water, or the air, but it seemed a living, moving thing that encompassed her. She remembered the day they arrived at the small harbour at the base of the Santorini cliffs, the smell of the sea and the sound of the waves crashing on the rocks. The donkeys were waiting on the beach to carry them up the hill into the town of Fira. One of the guides had a small transistor radio attached to his basket, and through the tiny speaker came the sound of Van Morrison singing "Brown-Eyed Girl," distorted with static. She and Oliver smiled to each other, as the airwaves provided this only reminder of their other life.

Chapter 6

UNFORTUNATELY, CLAIRE'S LOVE FOR OLIVER AND GREECE weren't strong enough to overcome her desire for home. She was no longer sleeping soundly, and for some reason she was becoming fiercely homesick, as if she could sense that something was wrong. Soon after she started having these feelings, she received the letter about the family tragedy. Her grandparents had both been killed in a fire in their home. A grief-stricken Claire could only think to return home as soon as she could make arrangements. Oliver refused to return with her, questioning why she needed to go—after all, they were no longer alive, and there was nothing she could do for them. She felt that this was heartless, and she wanted her family. Most of all, Claire wanted to see Paul.

So, through tears and anger, she made her preparations without Oliver. He remained silent throughout her packing and planning, all the while looking lost and confused. He stood at the harbour, watching as she boarded the ferry that took her to Pireas. Oliver didn't go with her to the airport, instead asking their friend Stavros to take her. It was a gut-wrenching trip back to Canada, alone. If she had been in the mood, Clara Perova, Musical Director Extraordinaire would have played

Demis Roussos's mournful "Goodbye My Love Goodbye."

Coming home proved more a challenge than she ever could have prepared for, as she now felt like an intruder in her own home. In true Perova fashion, her mother somehow managed to make her feel like she should have been here when the fire happened, as if she could have somehow prevented the tragedy. As quickly as she could, Claire found a job with a local real estate firm and found a small apartment above a video store in a strip-mall. This would be very temporary, she told herself, Anything to avoid living in her parents' house. Claire was unaccustomed to the aloneness she was feeling. Each night, when she closed her eyes, she still sensed the familiarity of Oliver, of his smell, and the sound of his voice. These events had unfolded far too quickly.

Did home always look like this or had it changed? Or was it she who had changed? Here there was noise, and traffic, and discontented people. The sound of lapping water had been replaced with honking car horns and the rumbling of trains. Not to mention that every time she heard "So Long Marianne" by Leonard Cohen, she started to cry. The little things surprised her too, like using microwaves and toasters, and learning to wear shoes and stockings again.

Everyone she knew seemed to have disappeared into the framework of the town, caught up in lives she no longer felt a part of. She had become a stranger in her own land, a land where the streets played no music. Paul and Claire spent a great deal of time together during this period. He had grown up in the years that she was gone, both emotionally and physically. At six feet, he stood five inches above her. Paul was very quiet and soft spoken, but he had a wicked sense of humour.

When he wore his glasses, he looked like Ilya Kuryakin, David McCallum's character in "The Man from Uncle." Paul also shared Claire's piercing blue eyes.

Claire and her mother rapidly returned to their normal, strained relationship, and her father was the perpetual peace-keeper. Claire could see her mother through different eyes now, and her perceptions were that her mother envied her children's independence, youth, and free choices—the things she had been robbed of. Her life had been stripped away by a war and the need to relocate across an ocean, away from everything that was familiar. It couldn't have been easy, as she had not made these decisions. But communication was not a strong point, so much of this was left to inference. After a few months of acclimation and reflecting on everything that had happened, Claire slowly started moving forward.

A month had passed before she felt ready to drive past her grandparent's home. It had been so badly damaged that the property was sold as a lot rather than a structure. The new buyers were re-building their new house from the existing frame of the old one, but they must have run into either finan-cial or zoning difficulties, because the work had been stalled. When Claire drove to the property, she felt her heart sink. She parked her car and walked across the street to the unfinished eyesore that stood before her.

In her mind, she pictured the house as it was. The back porch with the shingled roof, the little detached garage where her grandfather kept all of his tools, him lawnmower and his little glass jars filled with nuts and bolts. They were all gone. In their place stood an oversized, partially finished house. The exterior was covered with vapour board sheathing and had no finish on it. Peeking in the windows, Claire saw that the place had been gutted. Nothing looked the same, not a single memory remained. There was now a family room where the kitchen had once been.

Even the yard, which she remembered as having been so big, was now completely grown over with weeds, ivy, and dead trees. The morning glories, which her grandmother had carefully confined to a small plot by the back entrance, were now evident in every part of the yard. Claire imagined that they were searching for her grandmother; the only living essence to show that she had ever been there. There was no trace whatsoever of the vegetable garden. Was there ever room for one in this seemingly small area?

After the funeral, Claire's parents had come back to the house to see if anything salvageable remained. Sifting through the ash, they had miraculously uncovered her grandfather's metal case, which held his long-playing vinyl records. All 35 of them had been spared, except for a few that were slightly warped from the heat. They had saved for the records Claire, and she would be eternally grateful for that. Small flowered pots and jars, and her grandmother's favourite cast iron pans, were the only other things that remained. Claire's heart broke for her grandparents and for how she could never regain what she had lost.

Chapter 7

A YEAR LATER, PAUL, NOW 25, MET A LOVELY ENGLISH GIRL named Suki, who was in Canada working in a foreign exchange program. They were inseparable during her two-year stay, so when he followed her back to Britain, nobody was overly surprised. Suki's family flew over from London and gave them a fitting send-off with a lovely wedding at the Simcoe Lake Resort. They spared no expense for Paul and their daughter. All the tables were decorated in flowing white covers with red rose petals strewn across them. They had written their own vows, and the ceremony was simple yet elegant. It was a very heartfelt and touching celebration.

The evening ended with a bizarre phenomenon. June bugs surrounded the windowed reception hall while the guests were inside. They came from nowhere, like locusts, buzzing around in the air, cramming towards the light. Anyone who attempted to leave the building to make a mad dash for their car was immediately covered in the frantic, buzzing bugs, which would embed themselves in hair and turned into a crunchy carpet underfoot. Although the bugs are known to come out of the ground to mate, seeing them in these numbers was inconceivable.

People stood inside in horror, watching them cover the windows and streetlights, delaying their departure until the very last moment. One of the wedding guests stood up and enthusiastically announced that in some cultures, the beetle is often seen as a lucky charm. Apparently, they are a symbol of transformation and luck. He went on to describe them as stable creatures that represent constant progress and full dedication. No one in the room was enjoying this spectacle more than he was, but people cheered and applauded him.

Claire remembered her attempt to dash to her car without carrying bugs into it, Paul watching her through the window and laughing. "The hell with lucky charms," she had muttered. "Just get me away from these creepy bugs."

Oddly enough, the following morning, not a bug was to be seen anywhere.

Paul and Suki moved to Yorkshire two weeks later, and they took their time settling into family life. Then, one morning Claire's phone rang, and it was Paul announcing that he and Suki were pregnant. Claire knew that he was now cemented into his new life, and she would miss him terribly. He had become a necessary part of her life. After their son was born, Paul moved his family to a small rented house in Derbyshire in the village of Bakewell, where he would begin his training as a baker, producing the famous Bakewell Tarts. Her little brother had found his element. It was now Claire's turn to remain behind and yearn for her sibling, although she was convinced this was the right place for her to be.

Claire's connection with Kate began at Paul's wedding. She would never forget that time, as it was also the year that John Lennon was murdered on his doorstep. She and Kate got involved in deep conversation about the murder, and they began to realize that they had a lot in common and that they actually liked each other. Kate confided to Claire that she was divorcing Peter, and so the conversations veered to their individual separations and of possibilities that their futures now held for them.

A year later, Claire learned that her parents, who had long been retired, decided to move west to a coastal area near Vancouver. Their plan was to sell everything and drive across the country, shipping those few items that wouldn't fit in the car. This came as a blow, as Claire was just getting over the feeling of losing Paul. Nonetheless, she assisted them with the sale of their home and when moving day arrived, she hugged them tightly. She promised to visit one day. Her mother looked happy and for that, Claire was thankful.

Around the same time, Claire had started working with Kate, who was now officially divorced from Peter. Claire and Kate seemed to be at a similar crossroads in their lives, both looking for a way to move on. That's when Claire found this great house on the west side, and her first thought was to approach Kate. Before long, they had both moved into a newer split level home on a hill. Kate by then had left the firm and had begun work at the courts, as a Notary Public. So, at thirty, Claire had become totally upbeat, finding a new drive and optimism. It had been a very difficult decision to leave Oliver in Greece, but it still felt like it was for the best.

Claire thrived on the security and familiarity of things around her. She had no particular desire to uproot herself and leave all of her comforts behind. In the wake of all of her losses over the past few years, she was just beginning to re-discover herself. Despite of, or *because* of, the size of her town, she found herself content with her life. Kate was now her family.

By contrast, Will didn't live in town and had always said that he had very little desire to spend any more time there than was necessary. He had lived further beyond the borders of the town in what was referred to as the boonies. It was essentially a village, just over the county line and in a different jurisdiction, although it was near enough to still be considered an extension of the town. Claire recalled him saying that he had always loved open spaces. His small mechanics shop was situated halfway between his home and the town center, so he was inclined to spend most of his time between those two locations. His customers generally took their vehicles to him, and he was rarely seen elsewhere.

This was not a huge town, and events of any magnitude were highly unusual. The news of Will's death reverberated through the town, but then it seemed to blow over just as fast, so the case very quickly went dead. It was simply assumed that Will had slipped and fell into the pond, an unfortunate accident. There appeared to be no indication of foul play. The person who seemed closest to him was his partner, Glen, and he had been unable to shed any more light on what might have happened. This still didn't sit well with Claire. His death shook her in a profound way that she couldn't explain.

It was well past midnight, and though Claire had gone to bed at 10:00, she was still awake. She used to relish lying like this, mulling over her day and losing herself in thought. It seemed that Claire couldn't escape living close to the train tracks, as she did while growing up. As a child, she would wait for the rhythmic clicks and clacks when the trains came by.

It was always a sure thing that the gentle rumbling and the forlorn whistle would lull her to sleep. But tonight, as the din approached, it was an intrusion. The trains sounded angry and imposing. She pulled the covers over her head and eventually fell sleep.

Chapter 8

WEEKS PASSED AND STILL NO BREAKING NEWS, AS WAS typical with media in the suburbs. The only follow-up by the press was the funeral notice. With a little prompting, Kate accompanied Claire to Will's memorial service. Since Will as well-known through his business, it was no surprise that the room was filled with people from all walks of life. Claire recognized Glen, the man who came to the dance with Will the night she met him. She heard someone say that he was a mechanic who ran Will's shop with him. Attending this service revealed the man she never knew.

Kate quietly mingled among some people she recognized, while Claire sat and waited for her. When she returned, it was with new information about Will. It appeared that he had been previously married and had a fifteen-year-old daughter. They married when they were in their early twenties and the union had lasted just over seven years. Apparently, Will's ex-wife had been asked to come by some of his friends, since she was the only family that would be representing the deceased. She had agreed with apprehension. When the service began a few moments later, the reluctant ex-wife did speak, albeit briefly. Her robotic scripted eulogy focused mainly on Will's role in the community. She lowered her paper and, in the same monotone fashion, gave her condolences to anyone who was affected by his demise. Her speech was colourless, and she sat down quickly. Will's daughter sat quietly and appeared disinterested. It struck Claire as odd that these two people displayed little or no emotion regarding the death of a man who was once a major part of their lives. Also odd was the fact that they didn't mingle with any of the guests. Claire sensed that they would have preferred to be anywhere but here.

Despite the unlikelihood that anyone knew of her relationship with Will, Claire couldn't help but notice one man who seemed to be eyeing her with curiosity. She tried to make herself look small in her seat.

Beside her, Kate watched her behavior and finally whispered, "What the hell is wrong with you? You're acting weird."

Claire answered, "I think someone is watching me." Kate looked at her like she was losing her mind and rolled her eyes.

When the service was over and everyone was standing outside saying their hellos and goodbyes, Claire leaned over to Kate.

"I'm not kidding, Kate. That man is definitely watching me. He just followed us outside. Just do me a favor and hang back until after I pull out—I want to see if he will follow me out on to the road."

"Oh, for Chrissake, Claire! Who are you now? Nancy Drew?"

"Please just humor me, Kate."

With obvious displeasure, Kate agreed. Claire made her way to her car. She started the ignition and slowly drove off, her eyes on her rear-view mirror. How she wished that Ben were here with her now.

Kate came in not far behind her and simply said, "I'm sorry, Claire—no boogeymen. Nobody pulled out after you." She threw her handbag on the chair and said, "I'm tired and I'm going upstairs now. See you tomorrow."

Over the next few weeks, Claire and Kate made a point of taking at least a superficial glance at every newspaper and listening to the radio whenever they could, waiting for any kind of news. Will wasn't a high-profile person, so there was very little interest. Kate had heard something about a man who lived on the adjoining farm being questioned. Could this be the place with the horses? Up until now, there had been nothing of note, so when she saw an article in the newspaper, she took it as a positive sign.

"I suppose that something is better than nothing," Kate said to Claire as she handed her the paper. There, at the bottom of the article, Claire saw a picture of a man she recognized. It was the man who was watching her at the memorial service! The article identified him as Wolfgang Krueger.

Claire exclaimed, "Kate, this is the man who was watching me at the memorial! Look, it says he was Will's neighbour. I know of him, he's the horse guy!" It says he may or may not have witnessed something leading up to Will's drowning." Claire felt the blood drain out of her face. How did he know who she was, and why had he been watching her?

"Kate, I just remembered something that Will had told me," she continued. "I was at the cottage, and it was windy, and the horses acting up. We lay in bed listening to this guy, who had come outside to check on them. We could hear his voice, and he sounded distressed. I asked Will if he thought there might be a problem and whether he wanted to go out and check if everything was okay. He said something to the effect of, 'Trust me, it's better that I don't go out there if Wolf is around. There are things about him that make me uneasy.' I just never thought about it again. It didn't seem important."

Kate looked at her and, with some concern in her voice, said, "Claire, maybe it's time you just let this go. You are beginning to conceptualize all kinds of bizarre scenarios. Stop looking for shit that might not be there. Your imagination is starting to run away with you." She softened her tone before adding, "Hey look, even if any of this was your problem, I don't think it is now. And to be quite honest, you hardly knew Will at all, right?" With that, she rose from the sofa and left the room.

Claire was left with her thoughts, which had taken her back to a particular day at Will's cottage. She pictured the horses, watching them over the fence, gently snorting. She had been snapping some photographs earlier, but she was now seated under a tree shaded from the sun. She was sipping her wine, occasionally looking over at Will as he focused on nothing in particular. He was sitting on a rock, throwing stones into the pond as he hummed some sort of tune, seemingly without a care in the world.

Chapter 9

EARLY THE FOLLOWING MORNING, KATE DELUCA GOT UP to go for a run. After tying her hair back with a turquoise scrunchie, she donned her matching leg warmers, more for style than warmth, and headed out the door. Her job offered her some flexibility, and this morning was one of those times. Kate worked not only as a Notary Public but occasionally as a freelance Court Reporter. She liked her work, but although she was diligent and capable, she didn't feel as driven as Claire. She treasured these opportunities to not think about the job and get out when the weather was decent. This morning's route was one of her favourites.

From their home, the road wound down the hill in a gentle curve, over the train tracks and past the lake. This was not a true lake, but rather a river that ran through 5 counties, from south to north, emptying into Cook's Bay. The section of the river that came through town was naturally very wide, having twice been graded to widen it, further giving it the appearance of a lake. Over the years, park-like areas were constructed on either side of the water, with winding paths leading from the parking lots to benches and picnic tables, giving people a green place to go within the boundaries of town.

Next came the barbecue pits, bike trails, and gazebos. Flocks of ducks, geese, and swans began to make this space their home, as it provided the grassy areas and water that they loved. The entire project had been a welcomed and much-loved addition to the community. Be it a quick lunch break or a day's outing, it became a very well-used space. Often, the local high school students would retreat there after their classes to sit in the grass and play guitars or eat leftover lunches. The biggest problem the town planning committee now faced was getting rid of goose droppings.

Each time she ran by this spot, Kate was reminded of the day her cousin died on that lake. It would have been six years ago this June. It had happened on the year of "Operation Soap." This so-called Operations was a scandalous series of raids conducted by police in Toronto against four gay bathhouses in the city, which took place that February. It was a major event, staying in the headlines for weeks. The lingering aftermath for those who were arrested was horrific, and it left a very bad feeling throughout the county. Most thought the police should let people be, since they weren't hurting anyone.

The papers said that he raids were a result of six months of undercover work into alleged sex work and other "indecent acts." Most of those arrested were found innocent of baseless charges. Some of those men went away in shame, and many that lived locally stayed to themselves and had all but become forgotten over time. The actual arrests did more harm than good.

But these raids marked a turning point for Toronto's gay community, as the protests that followed indicated they would no longer endure derogatory treatment from the police and the media. Those events also gave birth to the Coming Together Parade, held for Gay and Lesbian rights, although Toronto's own mayor refused to proclaim this event as Lesbian and Gay Pride Week. It seemed that for every step forward, someone would take them another step back. Kate loved these parades. She recognized the importance they held in society. Her motto was simply, "Leave people alone." Why was it that people's differences made them bad? Anyway, this was cause to observe, and it now coincided annually with her cousin's death, forever marking it as a personal remembrance.

Kate ran to the north end of the lake to where it narrowed again, and then she circled to the right to ascend from the other side back to the house. She realized that she was not at her best today, and she could feel the tightness in her calves. She decided to cut through the lane, which would shorten the run by half a kilometer. The town had begun to wake up, and the traffic was intensifying as people were leaving their homes to start the day.

Nearing the house, she saw Claire drive by, on her way out. She tried to wave and grab her attention. But at that moment she spotted something else, and her hand quickly went down. Not far behind was another car, and a fleeting glimpse of the driver alarmed her. He looked an awful lot like that man, Wolf.

Chapter 10

Claire was caught off guard by an early-morning phone call from her colleague, Bert. She had just stepped out of the shower and had run to the phone draped in only a towel.

"Good morning Bert," answered Claire, in as cheerful a voice as she could manage.

Bert Ostman was a broker partner in Claire's building, but he wasn't the most prized member of the staff. He had a roughness to him that was hard to get around. Bert hailed from a place called Abbotsford, somewhere on the West Coast. He married his high school sweetheart shortly after graduating. She was also from his home country of Turkey, and he felt blessed to have found her. Their life became a bit difficult as the Vancouver economy began to slip, eventually affecting the Fraser Valley region as well, where Bert lived. The province fell victim to major political unrest and troubling labour disruptions, and it became apparent that they were heading for a recession. So, rather than stay and deal with an unstable economy, he followed a job opportunity out east to be a partner at this company.

Bert looked like he was in his fifties, but it was difficult to tell. He had a fleshy face and a rotund physique. Although he was a very sharp dresser, it didn't seem enough to compensate for his lack of decorum. His disposition was such that capable as he was, people preferred to deal with him at a healthy distance. His vocal expressions alone drove people a step or two back. Still, he was good at his job, he was good to Claire, and their establishment was one of prominence and respectability.

"Hey Claire," said Bert in his hoarse, gruff voice.

She held the receiver a few inches from her ear, as the man's voice projected loudly through the telephone.

"I think you were planning on being somewhere this morning—wasn't there a listing you were due to shoot today? The agent called looking for you."

"Damn!" she mumbled under her breath. Now was not the time to be slipping.

"Bert, can you please call him back and tell him I'm on my way?"

She gathered her gear and made her way over to the client's house.

Claire had a great appreciation of her job. Back when she was still contemplating her career options, she would often encounter former classmates, who were by then practically unrecognizable. She would watch as these portly women dragged their grimy-faced youngsters through the shopping malls and bargain stores. These were young girls who had had such promise, now victims of the small-town mentality—in short: meet a boy, get married, and become pregnant.

Claire and Paul had fought hard to avoid the pitfalls of small-town life. Claire had never married or had children, and she has never regretted that decision. The responsibility of raising a family frightened her. Paul was wise to leave and create the life he wanted for himself. As for Claire, she was happy that she came back to stay, and she had set personal goals based on what she wanted and not on what others thought she should do.

Thursday came quickly, and the week had proved to be a busy one. Claire didn't seem to have much time for anything else, which nicely gave her a chance to focus on the tasks at hand. As the week was nearing a close, Claire returned to the office late one morning to meet with Bert. They discussed clients for a short time, going over orders and figures until Bert got up and stretched, saying he'd love to go get a coffee.

Together, they went outside and leisurely made their way down Main Street to their favourite coffee shop. This was usually a guise to allow time for Bert to grab a few puffs of his cigarette, and he was never in a hurry in these moments. His smoking was just one more thing that made him unapproachable in her eyes. As they strolled on in the soft sunlight, she noticed Wolf walking up the opposite side of the street and disappearing around the corner.

"Bert!" she practically shouted. "Quick—see that man? Do you know who he is?"

Before Bert could react, the man was gone.

Chapter 11

OF LATE, AS CLAIRE PREPARED FOR SLEEP, HER THOUGHTS always returned to Will. What really happened the night he died? There was no evidence of foul play, yet there seemed to be little effort to develop new theories. He didn't strike her as a heavy drinker, so the idea of him having an inebriated tumble seemed unlikely. Was anybody trying to find out what happened?

Will had lived there for many years, and he knew the lay of the land like the back of his hand. So, to suggest that he somehow missed a step or tripped seemed suspect. Apparently, the area where he was found was at the back of the pond, which was completely overgrown with bramble and thorn. There was no bank on that rocky side and on her visits there, the area looked like it had never been tended. She wondered why he would have been on that side.

A mighty gust of wind blew through the maple trees beside her house, the sound jolting her upright to attention. Claire got up to close the window. An eerie feeling overcame her as she drifted back to sleep. She dreamed of Oliver for the first time in years. He was smiling at her while the sun was shining on his face. She woke early, thinking she was back in Greece.

Half asleep, she felt the area beside her to see if he was there. It was a few moments later, when she was wide-awake, that she was struck with the realization Will reminded her of Oliver. That could be where the attraction began. This realization pissed her off.

Claire sipped her coffee and said good morning to Kate, who had just come down the stairs. It wasn't typical for her to get up before Kate, and they rarely had coffee at the same time. They shared very little dialogue, as Claire was still waking up and thinking of what her day would bring. Kate looked annoyingly fresh and perky. Mumbling goodbye her friend, Claire gathered her things and left.

Claire had a photoshoot this morning. Oddly enough, it was very close to where Will ran his small business. A developer had purchased two parcels of land on the edge of town and was converting them to estate homes on half-acre lots. Rocky Ridge Estates was to be the new name. She was checking out the early phase, as she had been commissioned to take some photos for their sales campaign. Although she was only asked to overlook the rough landscaping around the perimeter, she planned to include photos, as she felt that those who preferred a more natural landscape might find it very appealing.

Driving up to the site, she was impressed with what she saw. Originally, the location for Rocky Ridge Estates had drawn a lot of skepticism and disapproval from the public. The new Mayor, who was elected in 1983, faced a major drop in approval ratings he backed this project two years later, when it looked like the market was going crashing.

Now that she was here, Claire saw that clearing the land had opened some spectacular vistas. Even though it was located only a short distance from the center of town, it felt secluded. The entrance to the estates opened to four lanes and displayed a rock formation with cascading water and appropriate landscaping, allowing for every possible colour of vegetation. This was a very tasteful project and it had gained much-needed approval.

Driving into the area, Claire noticed that the leaves on the boulevard trees had started turning, and it added to the spectacle. The main road was lined with stately, mature trees, whereas these were considerably smaller, having been recently planted. Claire could picture what the area would look like once these trees grew, adding continuity to the drive into the complex. Hopefully, these homes could still sell at a decent price and would not go for a loss. She parked, opened her trunk, and with her usual verve, prepared herself for the project.

Once she had set up her tripod and pulled out her site plan, she was fully engaged in her task. The ground where she stood was fairly level, and she had a good range of view. She selected a good wide-angle lens and her linear and UV filters. This would be the perfect place to view the upcoming hot air balloon festival, she noted. She looked up at the blue sky and smelled the breeze. She had a good feeling for the first time in a few weeks. It was the perfect day to be out here working, relieving her of thoughts of Will.

Chapter 12

Maria Dieno was the daughter of an immigrant couple, Jorge and Teresa, who had arrived in Canada from in Argentina. They moved into the house next door to Will's in 1967, when Maria was just 11 years old. The street ended against a beautiful forest of maple trees. It was an ideal place for family strolls or getting the dogs out for a run. By the time the road reached Will and Jorge's homes, it was just gravel— the pavement ended about half a kilometre back. It seemed out of the way to some, but to those who lived there, it was the perfect distance from town.

Maria was her parents' golden child, since they lost their youngest daughter shortly before they began the journey north. The poor girl had lost her battle with Fifths Disease. Teresa and Jorge had an extremely difficult time dealing with her death, and the ache of her loss was constant. The ensuing journey north and adjusting to life away from their country also took its toll on them. The most prominent obstacle was the hardship of learning a new language. They were a modest family that kept their lives to themselves. Jorge supported his family by doing carpentry jobs around town, while Teresa offered the odd house-cleaning service before landing a permanent cleaning job for a small privately owned nursing home.

Will had grown to know the family quite well, and it became a common occurrence to find him sitting outside with Jorge, having long talks. When Will had moved out and married, he returned frequently to spend time with his aging mom, who still lived next door. These visits with Jorge always continued. When Will's mother finally passed away, and the house was sold, there was no longer reason for Will to be on that side of town, so it was only on the occasion of Jorge needing his help did he ever out venture that way.

Rumor had it that a year after their daughter Maria graduated, she went to live in Toronto with a South American friend, a girl named Elyse. Upon returning to the family home nearly three years later, Maria was rarely seen. Her mother did her shopping, and one could occasionally get a glimpse of the reclusive Maria in the yard, donned in a kerchief and sunglasses. It was very bizarre behavior for a young woman.

Before Claire left for university, she and Paul would sometimes ride their bicycles this way, past the gravel road to the horse farm that lay beyond. It had always been her dream to have a horse of her own. This idea had captivated her since she was very young. On rare occasions, the man at the ranch would show her and Paul how to saddle up a couple of the horses and let them take the animals out for an hour or so. He had taught them how to tighten the girth by adding a gentle kick to the horse's belly, so they would let their air out—a practice that was more myth than fact, as she learned years later. Often, when they returned to the stable, the owner would be occupied somewhere on the other end of the ranch.

This gave them a great sense of responsibility, as now it was up them to unsaddle the horses and put the tack away before brushing them down and putting them back in the paddock. It was on these outings that Claire had her first glimpses of Will and of the Dieno family.

They would occasionally spot Maria walking the family dog along the gravel path that followed the road. It was certainly puzzling, this girl with a mysterious story. What had caused her reclusive behaviour? There were as was typical a small handful of people who loved to speculate, but for the most part the Dienos were left alone. Few knew the family, and fewer thought much about it. People have their own struggles and lives to deal with without bothering about others.

When Claire also moved away from the family home, her mind invariably turned to other things, so thoughts of her old neighborhood rarely crossed her mind. Life never stays the same for any of us, and it can sometimes move far too quickly. The things that we think we could never do without become tucked so far back in our minds, almost like they never existed. We find other things that we can no longer do without.

Chapter 13

THE MORNING WAS UNSEASONABLY COOL. CLAIRE PARKED behind her office and wrapped her sweater a little tighter as she made her way out to the main street. Walking briskly, she gazed up at the sky. It was a lovely morning, very sunny. Claire was the kind of person who always paid attention to the weather. She loved how the sights and smells of each season aroused new senses. She didn't mind the rain but disliked the very hot days. On this day, she could see few people on the street, as it was still quite early.

On the Main Street, every lamppost contained a hanging basket, each filled with an assortment of colourful flowers. Even though summer seemed to be ending, these baskets were still spilling over with an abundance of blooms. And with the help of the breeze, bloom petals were covering the windshields of the parked cars in a celebratory fashion. It excited her to think of autumn, with the changing leaves and cozy fireplaces.

Taking her place in the coffee line, Claire stood in the queue beside a woman whom she couldn't quite place, until she recognized her as having been at Will's memorial service. They exchanged a few pleasantries and, after glancing at each other numerous times in vague recognition, Claire suddenly remembered that she was Will's ex-wife. Turning to the woman with a smile and a lead-in, she introduced herself as someone who had been at Will's memorial service. The woman smiled back and introduced herself as Bonnie.

Claire stood quietly by her while she placed her order, unsure what else to say. Once she had her order, she turned to Claire with a goodbye and disappeared into the atrium.

Frustrated and wanting to act fast, Claire ordered her coffee and, as soon as it was poured, she grabbed her cup and hurried in to see where the woman had gone. She knew that she had promised Kate that she would drop the whole thing, but she couldn't help herself.

As soon as Claire rounded the corner, she saw Bonnie seated alone by the window. Claire took a deep breath and, with a daring move, approached the table.

"There are no seats left. Would you mind if I joined you for a few moments?"

"I don't know what we would have to chat about, we don't really know each other," was Bonnie's cautious, almost brusque reply.

"I won't stay long, honestly."

"I do know who you are. You are the person who was seeing Willie before he died. A friend of his pointed you out to me at the service."

"I am sorry for your loss, it must have been especially hard on your daughter," said Claire, as she quickly sat down without waiting to be invited.

With a tragic laugh, Bonnie said, "It was no loss, trust me. The wretched man is dead, but he's been dead to me for quite some time."

"What could have been so bad? I understand you've been apart for a long time now, yet you still seem so angry."

"Yes, we divorced six years ago." She let out a huge sigh, resigning herself to answer Claire. She then continued, slowly at first. "Some things you never get over and let me tell you, we were so broken, I can't believe I put up with it for so long."

Claire sat quietly, afraid to say anything, not wanting to discourage Bonnie from talking. After a pause, Bonnie relaxed, and for some reason she decided to continue telling Claire about Will.

"You are mourning. You miss him? Well, you shouldn't. He wasn't worth it. You see, there was this ongoing relationship—an interminably disgusting affair—and it went on for 10 years. The sick part is that I stayed for the first four, until the marriage finally ended. The affair was with a woman eleven years his senior, named Daniela Conti. She is the wife of an Italian restaurant owner, have you heard of them?"

Claire nodded, "They own a restaurant and a small cafe, is that right?"

"Yes, that's it. The husband, Tony, is this smarmy, greasy low-life. He has always seemed to me like a gangster. He spends a lot of time in Toronto, apparently mixed up in the running of some nightclubs—The Cabana and The Zone. I think he might be involved in drugs, or girls, or both. The clubs have never been linked to anything specific, but there have always been stories, and I think sometimes people know more than cops, for all their apparent cleverness. And we all know the police can be bribed. It's a pity that he's never been linked to anything."

"So, I guess it's safe to say that Tony and Daniela are not the picture perfect married couple," offered Claire.

Bonnie nodded, "Far from it. I'd hate to be a fly on the wall in their home."

Bonnie took a sip of her coffee before continuing, having relaxed considerably. Claire guessed it might be doing this woman good to talk about it.

"Well anyway, Daniela told Willie that if he ever tried to break off their affair, she would have his legs broken. This was according to Willie, and I had no interest in probing to find out if it was true. Willie seemed to love that twisted kind of possession, and he had no intention of ending their relationship. Yes, he even said that to me. He broke my heart."

Bonnie laughed a little, before adding, "When I actually stop and think about it, I was just as pathetic for accepting it. Willie seemed so totally intoxicated with this woman, he warned me to keep my mouth shut because it could hurt us all. I had a young child, I wasn't working, and I didn't want the shame. I just waited until he left me."

Claire interjected, "Hey, you were only doing what you needed to do at the time. You were surviving."

"Thank you, I'll take that," acknowledged Bonnie with a smile. "When he finally left, Daniela set Willie up in his lovely little cabin. It was her way of keeping her eye on him—a toy in the closet for whenever she wanted to play."

Claire sat there, wondering to herself if this was still going on during her brief time with Will. "Do you happen to know when their affair ended?" she asked Bonnie.

"As far as I know, it ended the day that Willie died," she said looking straight at Claire. "So, I guess he didn't tell you."

Chapter 14

"ACCORDING TO LOCAL GOSSIP, TONY WAS RARELY AROUND. From what I could tell, she and Willie were always very discreet. So discreet that at first, even I was not aware, idiot that I am. When Willie moved out, he went to a fairly isolated place, so nobody would ever see her coming and going. And I think she knew some pretty creepy people, given Tony's line of work. It was rumored that he left a few goons around the restaurants to look out for her.

"So, you think she paid for Will's cottage?"

"I don't think he could have afforded it on his own. He was a small business mechanic who had bills and needed to pay child support. Speaking of which, he hadn't seen his daughter in years."

Claire had never heard of a man not wanting to see his child.

Bonnie continued, "Anyway, Willie obviously didn't take her threats to heart, even though he made no effort to end the relationship. I think he almost found it amusing. But like I said, it's because he seemed to thrive on her neediness. It made him feel significant in some sick way. Plus, there was the fact that she lavished him with gifts. His new truck, for example. It struck me as odd that a restaurant such as Tony's could be lucrative enough to afford his wife anything she wanted."

This conversation was making Claire feel uneasy. She now

understood why Bonnie had been reluctant to speak with her, and she worried that she had pushed the poor woman to say more than she had intended.

"Bonnie, I really appreciate you talking to me. It must have taken a lot for you to open up to me about all of this. I did promise I wouldn't stay long, and now I really need to go to back to work," said Claire as she started to stand.

"Just one more thing," she grabbed Claire's arm. "I never would have told you any of this, but I'm telling you this now because I don't want you to forever think that you will miss out on something spectacular because Willie died."

Claire just stared at her in silence, at a total loss for words.

"But do you have any idea what might have happened to Will?"

"What do you mean?" said Bonnie. "It was just an accident."

Claire wasn't sure how to respond to that, so she decided not to mention that Will had called her two nights before. Perhaps it meant nothing, but she still seemed to be on some kind of truth-seeking mission, for reasons not even she could answer. And it likely would not interest Bonnie in the least.

"Yes, of course it was," agreed Claire.

Claire awkwardly said goodbye. This was not exactly a meeting of friends, and the conversation was quite unpleasant, so the parting was somewhat grim. She hadn't even touched on what kind of relationship the daughter had with Will.

"Oh, and it would be appreciated if this information didn't go any further than this coffee shop. If word got out about Willie and Daniela, I'm worried it could come back to me. I am assuming I was the only other person to know about this. Other than Glen at his shop, but Glen would never talk."

The two women again said goodbye, and Claire hurried

back to the office, feeling a bit nauseated. This was one of the most bizarre stories she had ever heard, outside of a movie or a book. It suddenly started to make sense that she and Will never saw each other in town. All of their meetings had been clandestine in nature, always in those cute little places where they could be anonymous—places like dark movie theatres, picnics in forested glens, or his cottage, away from prying eyes. What seemed endearing at the time now seemed repulsive.

What bothered Claire the most was the fact that Will had made her feel like she was special when in reality she was a sideline. Was the bed still warm from Daniela whenever she arrived? How soon after kissing her had he run to kiss Daniela? Claire was certainly feeling deceived, if not betrayed. It also worried her that she may have made Ben feel this way.

She went back in her mind and visualized Will's home, his clothing and belongings. His cottage was tastefully decorated—perhaps by a woman? This was something she failed to notice at the time, likely because it didn't seem important. Perhaps that was why she found it so attractive and appealing. His clothes, while casual, seemed high-end as well. Claire struggled to remember other things that would have given her clues, but none came to mind. She desperately felt like going home and crawling into bed with the covers over her head, but she had work to do, and she refused to allow Will to take over her thoughts.

Driving across town to her next appointment, she eventually pulled into the long circular driveway of a contemporary two-story house. The front gardens were impeccably groomed, complete with a small concrete water fountain. Set far back on the property, the first things Claire noticed were the massively oversized windows, adorned with decorative wooden shutters. The big wooden planter boxes were spilling over with colourful flowers. While the house only seemed to have two stories, it was very tall, likely due to high ceilings inside. The small winding path to the front door seemed to invitingly beckon visitors. Such homes rarely came up for sale in town, usually being handed down by generations.

Growing up, Claire could never have imagined herself inside a home on this side of town, even just for this purpose. Parking her car, she noticed that this place was not unlike that of Kate's parents, who invited her every year for Christmas dinner. She loved going there. They welcomed her warmly, always reminding her that she was family and that they loved seeing her. Kate's brother and sister treated her as if they were the ones who had a personal friendship with her, and her father would always promptly sit her down and insist she fill him in on all her news since her last visit. Kate's mother was a delightful woman who, although she enjoyed her wine a bit too much, had the biggest heart that she had ever known.

Claire sat in her car for a moment, viewing the exterior of the house. These owners had purchased space in a retirement community, and as they had no relatives willing to take this house over, they were forced to sell. Their biggest fear would be that it would be torn down to take maximum advantage of the lot size, and that two houses would be erected in its place.

With a sigh, Claire got out of the car and took off her colourful scarf. Slipping on her jacket and trying hard not to think of Will, she made her way to the rear of the car to get her camera. With feet that felt like lead in the wake of her encounter with Bonnie, she walked to the front door. She was grateful and pleasantly surprised when she was greeted by two smiling faces and the smell of freshly brewed coffee.

Chapter 15

THE DAYS WENT BY WITH NO NEWS, AND CLAIRE BEGAN TO fall back into the rhythm of everyday life. Much to her enjoyment, she had once again been given the opportunity to photoshoot the annual hot air balloon festival. Her photographs would cover the neighborhood feature story, promoting her town as a great place to live. This annual festival drew huge crowds, and it had much more to offer than balloons. There were balloon rides, food carts, face painting for the children, a small farmers' market where vendors would sell their preserves and fresh produce, macrame plant hangers, crocheting, and live music, courtesy of local bands. The festival would hold a special significance this year, as a Brit named Richard Branson and a Swede named Lindstrand made history only a few months prior, when they became the first men to cross the Atlantic in a hot air balloon. The event had inspired an attraction to hot air ballooning that previously didn't exist, or at least not to this extent.

Each year, the same highly trained balloon pilots and ground crew would take part, so they all came to know Claire on a first-name basis, except that they call her Bette Davis— because of her eyes. These pilots owned their own balloons, and they relied on highly skilled crew, so safety records were impeccable. Although personality wasn't a necessary part of their job, they were all brimming with it. "Hey, Bette!" they would greet her. Claire was looking forward to seeing everyone again.

But first, she and Kate were meeting in town so Kate could buy some new running shoes. Kate went through shoes very quickly, and she had carefully chosen this opportunity to once again try to convince Claire to start a running regime with her. Claire loved Kate and she enjoyed their time together, but she was hesitant about the running. The few times that Claire had tried it out, things didn't go well. First, there were the side stitches, and then there was the pain in her feet. She had never considered herself to be an athletic person, so by the third attempt, when she returned home with shortness of breath and more side stitches, she called it quits. She struggled for days with sore muscles, and she decided that she honestly couldn't understand the purpose of such activity. Claire was blessed with height and trimness, so fortunately she had never felt the need for vigorous activity aside from the occasional aerobics class at the community center. Kate could not convince her that jogging would be great for her stress. Her response was always the same: leave her to her walking because *running* would cause her stress. Nonetheless, Kate and Claire enjoyed these outings, and they usually ended with a trip to their favourite coffee shop for a latte and something sweet. This time, as per usual, Kate bought shoes, and Claire didn't.

Kate came from an affluent family, the youngest of three children. She grew up confident and kind, and as a result, she had been extremely popular in school. She was very athletic and had been an active member of every sports team. In her graduating year, she was nominated for valedictorian and, unlike Claire she definitely attended her prom. She had many offers for escorts and she chose Peter, who ultimately became her husband. She now thought of this as a bad choice.

Today was the second day of the festival and at dusk, the organizers had planned the annual Nightglow, where the tethered balloons would be fired up at dusk. Rather than simply letting the balloons rise, they were tethered at various heights along the ground. The balloons glowed like huge light bulbs for a spectacular visual display. This annual festival was one of the largest around, and the balloons here numbered into the hundreds. Claire and Kate would cover the afternoon events, but she needed to return by eight that evening to snap the Night Glow.

Walking through the grounds, Kate had just burst into hysterical laughter over something that Claire had said when a voice behind them called out, "Katie!" Two former classmates had recognized her and came to say hello. Jeannie, a tiny redhead, was asking about Paul, remembering the crush she had on him just before graduation. Claire was introduced as Paul's sister, and she found herself drawn into a conversation about Paul's new life in England.

Claire engaged in the conversation for a short while, but she quickly tired of the small talk. During a lull in conversation, she was able to excuse herself. With a friendly goodbye, she left the friends to their reminiscing while she wandered off eagerly to meet with the pilots. She loved the excited commotion of the activity around her. It made her senses come alive. Her eyes scoured the crowd in hopes of spotting Ben and

Adam. She kicked herself for not suggesting a meeting spot, if for no other reason than to just say hello. By late afternoon Claire headed home to freshen up and have a bite to eat. She had taken more than enough photos of the day's activities. Although it hadn't been a long day she feeling unusually tired. Finding herself unable to relax, she instead busied herself changing camera lenses and stocking up on film. She needed to keep her mind occupied.

Claire was back again at 7:45, just before dark. The entire crew had already had a very busy day, but the time had come for the Nightglow. Even during the day, the balloons were flown while still tethered to the ground. A balloon, although tied, is still considered to be a registered flying aircraft the second it leaves the ground. If they were untethered, there could be a real problem in allowing enough people to have rides, since there would be little control over where the balloon would come down due to manufacturing and wind factors. The ground crews would likely be forced to drive great distances to retrieve balloons, and the passengers would be stuck in the middle of nowhere with no ride back.

Claire had watched on many occasions as daytime crowds gathered excitedly around the balloons, tickets in hand, waiting for their turn to climb into the baskets. As the balloons were released, she could hear their screams of horror and delight as they were lifted from the ground. As appealing as this was, Claire preferred to keep both her feet on solid ground. It was bad enough that her head was often in the clouds.

Even tethered, these balloons could rise 100 feet, depending on the wind, so the rides were exciting. Tying the balloons in this fashion allowed them to go high and wide, and still be brought back safely to the same spot in a reasonable amount of time. These tethers are usually attached to the basket portion of the balloon.

During the Nightglow, the lines were all shortened to heights varying from four and seven feet, to create a dramatic effect. Also, the pilots would use what is called the "whisper burner," a liquid valve that replaced the blue flame main valve that they used during the day. This created a brilliant orange flame that was spectacular to see against the balloons in their beautifully assorted colours. These pilots' experience never failed to impress Claire. She loved to watch this and never tired of the images year after year. She ran a quick check with her light meter and adjusted the lens on her camera. This type of photography is what made her feel alive, and she felt her heart beat a little faster. For her, this was one of the most amazing sights her lens would ever capture. These photos would need no enhancing, although one could think that they had been touched up.

Chapter 16

TERESA DIENO WOKE UP, BUT SHE WAS NOT YET ABLE TO open her eyes. She had not slept well. She thought of her daughter, Maria, who had recently been going out after hardly speaking to them for three years. It had been a troubling time for Maria, which made it difficult for all of them. Maria's former roommate Elyse Berra was dead, yet her daughter wasn't saying anything about it. Although Maria swore that she knew nothing, Teresa always had her suspicions. The fact that Maria had become so secretive about her movements was particularly troubling.

Jorge had already left for the day. She heard the door shut and his truck start just as it was getting light. Teresa was grateful for this quiet time to herself. When Jorge was home, her time was spent making sure that everyone's emotions were in check. It was draining, as Jorge had become withdrawn, and she often heard him sighing, even moaning in his sleep. Jorge's way of dealing with things was to not deal with them. She was worried about him.

Teresa had recently taken a permanent job for a man named Larry Freye, who ran a nursing home. From staff gossip, Teresa learned that he was the brother of a man who was charged with the murder of a young boy named Mateo Berger in downtown Toronto. This murder sparked events that weighed heavily on the gay movement, as it shed a negative light on the gay community. Mateo had been sexually abused before he died, and the men responsible—including Larry's brother—had escaped out west. They were never brought to trial. Larry had grown up estranged from his brother, and he was sickened by all of the increased attention brought on by these events. Even though he was innocent, people looked at him differently because of his brother's actions. He and his wife opened their nursing home and disappeared into a modicum of anonymity. Those who worked for Larry sympathized with him and respected his privacy, as did Teresa. And she didn't mind that the residents were few and that the staff moved about slowly, with a resigned stoicism. She was simply grateful for the job, and she enjoyed her days out of the house.

What concerned Teresa was the timing of the deaths of Elyse and Mateo. It was the same month and the same year. The boy was sixteen, and Elyse was nineteen. She knew of no connection between the deaths, yet she felt sure that there was one. But try as she might, she could find nothing to tie these two events together. Her co-worker, Linda, told her that she wasn't thinking clearly, and that she should stop imagining things. The only reason she was thinking this way was because she worked for Larry, but that was not a real connection, no matter how you looked at it. Mateo just happened to be in the wrong place at the wrong time. His death was a sex crime.

The circumstances surrounding the death of Elyse were less sinister. After all, the papers said that her death appeared to have been brought on by her own actions. Teresa tried to be rational about this. But what if Elyse had known Mateo? What if they had met, either through work or through a friend? Or maybe Mateo knew her cousin, Dany. They were both from South America, so perhaps they frequented the same circles? Mateo could have come looking for Dany and found Elyse there instead. But they were dead, and Dany had disappeared, so there was no one to ask—except for Maria, and she wasn't talking. Teresa worried about what her daughter might know. Was there something she may have seen, or even done? The police said that Elyse's death was drug-related. Was her daughter on drugs? How could she tell? The girl simply would not talk, and to push her might drive her away.

She wondered if she had angered God, such that he took her eldest daughter Valeria and now was testing her faith again with her only remaining daughter. With Valeria, the circumstances were beyond her control. The poor child's frail body was not strong enough to stand up to the virus that ultimately took her life. But she felt that with Maria, she might have some control over the outcome and keep her daughter from harm. But who could help her?

Maria had become a different person since returning home. She and Elyse had always been responsible girls, mature for their ages, and although Jorge never warmed up to the idea of the girls living on their own, Teresa had encouraged it. She hoped that it would be a way to gain some independence and develop a sense of responsibility. But where did it go wrong? Now, Maria seemed old beyond her years, and she appeared tortured with this anguish.

Jorge would forever make her feel guilty for her encouragement, but she could never have imagined how badly events would unfold. Elyse's parents were also an issue. They had not spoken to Teresa and Jorge since the death of their daughter. This saddened her, since Jorge and Elyse's father were close, and Jorge felt the loss. Yet, she herself felt no culpability for the untimely death of Elyse. Her husband said that she might not feel that way had it been Maria and not Elyse who had died. Their small world was getting smaller.

All she could do was watch Maria and hope for her to return to her old self. It was more troubling that lately, Maria had been going out alone, saying nothing about where she was going or when she would be back. Teresa felt that she needed to talk to someone. The only person she could think of was a woman named Daniela, whom she had met through their neighbor, Will. Teresa had cleaned this woman's home for a little while. Perhaps she would talk to this her and ask for advice? Linda suggested that Teresa just leave it alone. What would Daniela possibly know about it? But Teresa would give it some thought, as she felt helpless doing nothing.

Chapter 17

On Saturday morning, as Claire rolled over in bed, she was awakened by the phone. She smiled when she heard the voice. It was Ben.

"This is a nice surprise, Ben." Claire felt remarkably light-hearted at hearing his voice on the line. "What a great start to the morning. You couldn't have called at a better time."

Claire had been hoping that she would run into Ben at the Balloon Festival, but the grounds were large and she was on assignment, so the likelihood was slim. She had been disappointed when she hadn't spotted him, as his would have been a welcome face.

"I called your office yesterday, and they told me you had gone home. I looked for you at the festival, but we were there very early. I was with my neighbor and his two kids, and the agenda included doing the face-painting thing. But don't worry, Fred and I didn't get our faces painted, just the kids! Then we had to eat hot dogs and cotton candy; it was pretty disgusting. I've had better days, but Adam had a good time."

Adam was Ben's son, a quiet little boy with big eyes and a bigger grin. He and Claire were slowly getting to know each other. She had always enjoyed the opportunity to accompany them for a walk in a park or the occasional lunch at Pirate Pete's. On the last few visits, quite by surprise, Adam had run over to give her a hug, slowly becoming more accustomed to having her around.

"I brought him home with this stuff smeared all over his face and mustard all over his clothes. I'm sure I would have preferred the festival from your perspective. I know you were busy and had a lot to do. I hope the day went well for you."

Claire laughed at Ben's description of his day. His world was so different from hers, and she enjoyed the contrast. "I was quite busy but I did look for you as well, Ben. I really hoped I'd run into you. I bought Adam a toy parachute." She had remembered that Ben had told her how much he loved parachutes. "I can give it to him next time I see him."

"That was very nice of you Claire., he will be thrilled." He went on to say, "and you have perfect timing! One of the reasons I'm calling is to say that Adam has been asking about you," Ben paused before continuing. "Actually he was asking if you would like to come to his birthday party next weekend."

"I wouldn't miss it for the world, Ben. Please tell Adam I am thrilled to be invited." Claire grabbed a pen and paper and wrote down the information as Ben then asked her how she was coping with things since they last spoke. She began by describing the day at the festival from her perspective. The day went too quickly and now it was over for another year.

"And on another note Ben, I think you are right about me getting too involved with what happened in relation to Will's death. I'm finding out things I don't want to know, and I feel as if I am getting drawn into something that I want no part of. I was hoping we could find time to talk about it."

"I'd be really happy to talk about that with you. I have tried not to ask, but I was waiting until you felt ready to bring up the subject. If it works with our schedules, we should try to meet up this week. Otherwise, let's talk at the party, Claire." She hung up the phone thinking about Ben, and how hard he was working at keeping life normal for his son. It took a lot of juggling even for two parents, yet he didn't seem to miss a beat doing it on his own.

After she and Ben had said their goodbyes, she slowly made her way down the stairs. Feeling very calm and clear-headed, she smiled to herself. Today would be a good day for putting on some music, and for developing her film from yesterday. Kate had been up before her, as there were crumbs on the counter beside a half-finished cup of coffee. She put on a fresh pot to brew and then headed outside to find her friend.

Chapter 18

THE BIRTHDAY PARTY WAS HELD AT THE KOSMIC KIDS. Upon entering the building, Claire placed the wrapped parachute on the pile with the other presents. It pleased her when Adam ran over to hug her, and he seemed more interested in her than in the gift. The gesture left her with an unfamiliar feeling of warmth inside. She looked over at Ben, who was smiling. This was the first time that she had ever been inside these walls, and she instantly hoped that it would be her last. It was loud enough with just the music and the beeping machines, but this was amplified by hordes of screaming little tykes. Looking around, it seemed as though the noise was simply one long scream suspended in the air—it didn't actually seem to be coming from any child in particular. She subconsciously made a face, but one sideways glance at Ben helped to turn the face into a smile. Once she became accustomed to the noise and had recovered from her initial reaction, she really did envy the wholesome, carefree innocence of children. Adam grabbed her hand and led her to his allotted area of the party room.

Five of Adam's little friends were there, ready to climb on the spaceships and shoot their lasers even before they had their space burgers and cookies. After a bit of socializing with the few other parents that were there, Ben caught Claire's attention and motioned to a quiet spot where they could go and sit for a spell. After Ben had assured himself that the kids were well occupied, he sat further back in his chair, relaxed, and smiled warmly.

"At last, a moment alone."

Clair looked at him and laughed, "Adam is delightful. Look at him, Ben. He's having the time of his life. And he's really sweet. He seems so calm and even-keeled, and he's not hyper like some of the kids here."

Ben laughed back, saying "It wasn't always like this. Now that Adam is six, I think he is beginning to understand and identify the more complex feelings that he goes through, and oddly, it's had a calming effect on him. He used to get angry, frustrated, and disappointed all at once. Now, he understands his emotions better, and he seems to take it all in stride. I'm not saying he's a model child, but he's so much better."

Ben leaned forward in his chair. "For example, he used to come home from school despondent about having to spend a few hours at daycare, where he would watch other mothers coming to pick their kids up. Now, he is more accepting of the fact that he doesn't have a mommy like the other kids do." Ben looked over at his son. "During this last year, he's finally stopped asking. And instead of worrying that he doesn't have a mom, he seems more worried that I don't have her either. Sometimes it's like he's already trying to take care of me."

"Ben, what did happen to Adam's mom? I hope you don't mind my prying," ventured Claire. It was a question she long wanted to ask.

"She left," began Ben. "She had a very hard time during pregnancy. The last four months almost killed her, with abdominal pain, always some bleeding, and a few infections. She also experienced back pain and visual problems. And then the delivery was a nightmare, to put it mildly. She didn't want to hold Adam when it was all over. She remained in the hospital for a week after—she was just traumatized. When I brought her home, she was disengaged. She had a hard time nursing, so we abandoned it for formula and a bottle."

He mused, "I guess when men disconnect from their kids, people will look at it as almost typical. When a woman does, there's a real stigma attached to it."

A scream interrupted their conversation. Ben jumped up to respond to a crying child who dropped her cookie. When he returned, he went on to say, "Then, one day she left. She didn't lose us—she left us. I don't know why, although I try to understand it. It would have been easier to understand if it was for a job, or for another man, or whatever. But she simply walked out the door. I had a nagging feeling that she found something better than Adam and me, but the truth is, she no longer felt able, or willing, to go on. She was simply depleted. Her mother told me that she moved to Manitoba, to her sister's, and I have no idea if she's still there.

My friends would say to me, "What kind of a mother leaves her kids?" Ben looked up at her. "But you know what? Some just do. It was way beyond my comprehension for a long time. I read stuff you know; I did a bit of research. For some reason, it seems to be happening a lot right now. Is this the new age of rebellion by young mothers? I don't know. But none of that matters now. That was over five years ago, and I doubt she's coming back any time soon, if ever."

Ben stood up to take Adam his cookies. "I don't know what's going on the world sometimes."

They both sat silent for a long time. Claire was twirling her straw and listening to Michael Jackson on the loudspeaker. Suddenly she looked up at Ben and said,

"Hey, are you ready for us to go away? I mean the three of us. I want us to go to England and visit Paul. I miss him so much, Ben. He writes often, trying to convince me to come and check out his corner of the world. My life has become a bit confusing, and I could use a distraction."

Smiling with a generous helping of levity he said, "Let's work on that, Claire."

"So, I should get out of here before the mad dash, Ben. Just let me go and say goodbye to Adam." Claire got out of her chair and wandered off to find the boy. She certainly didn't want to push the issue of going away with Ben and she wasn't certain where the comment had come from. It had just felt right at that moment. When she was ready, Ben took her by the hand and walked with her to where the cars were parked. As they said goodbye, he held her fiercely and kissed her gently.

Claire decided that any conversation about Will could wait for another time. As she drove away, she thought of Ben and the struggle he must have had raising Adam alone while maintaining a career. She was seeing Ben through new eyes. It was commendable that he had the ability to provide the time it took for nurturing Adam without the child feeling that he missed out somehow. She thought of how different this was from Will's relationship with his daughter.

Claire wondered if she could have handled the situation as

well as Ben had. She had yet to learn that kind of nurturing love; the kind of love that a parent has for a child. The kind they call 'unconditional love.' In the soundtrack of her musical genius, the song that came to her mind was "Beautiful Boy," by John Lennon.

Chapter 19

IT WAS TUESDAY, ANOTHER CLOUDY DAY. CLAIRE'S ARMS were loaded up with papers and camera equipment, and she headed towards the building when Bert pulled up beside her in his rusty brown Ford Explorer. He called over, "We need to talk, Claire. I hardly see you these days, and we need to schedule a meeting. Check your calendar and let me know when we can sit down." He went to the rear of his vehicle to take his things out of the trunk. "Things need to be discussed and strategies need to be developed, especially with another increase in interest rates and the glut of listings. This new developer will take a hit, and it scares me that we may go down with him."

This was Bert's idea of an actual conversation.

Without even waiting for a response, he turned his back and walked towards the door, ahead of her. Claire stood there in amazement as she struggled with her arms full, without so much as a "Can I hold the door for you?" from Bert. What the hell was this man's problem?

"Oh and hey," he called over his shoulder, "Ruth has a message for you from a woman named Maria Dieno. Do you know her?"

Claire muttered something back to him, knowing that he

was no longer listening to her by now. The only Maria Dieno she had heard of was Will's old neighbour, but why would she be calling her? As far as she knew, the woman was quite a recluse. Regardless, she would be sure to call her back.

After warmly greeting Ruth and the other office staff, Claire went to her workspace and laid out the file from the photoshoot she had completed at Rocky Ridge Estates. While she was concentrating on the work in front of her, there was still an active part of her brain that couldn't stop mulling over the information from the conversation she had with Bonnie, a few days prior. To have been caught in a situation like that took her by surprise. She was angry about the way that she had behaved with Will. It was totally out of character for her to run into this man's arms like a halfwit, with no apprehension or savvy.

Exactly what game was Will playing? He had no business getting involved with her when he appeared to have plenty of women problems already. She knew that she could only blame herself, as she hadn't exactly been distancing herself from the man that night. She did feel a bit embarrassed when she recollected her behavior, giggling like a complete moron. She couldn't figure out why she had held back from Ben, yet seemed to leap toward Will.

As she looked at the photo in front of her more closely, she suddenly noticed something that wasn't supposed to be there. It was a person, on the left, walking around to the front of the building. *This isn't right.* She couldn't use this in a promotional shot. Why didn't she notice this before? The person was not recognizable, as it was not a face shot, but she was sure it was a male. She couldn't crop him out, as she would lose a key element of the photo. She would, unfortunately need to go and re-shoot. This added to her growing frustration.

"What's wrong, Claire, are you alright?" Bert had heard her sigh and had come up beside her, without her noticing. She jumped. He had a habit of doing that, and Claire had no idea whether he did it on purpose or if the man just put her on edge.

"It's just that this picture needs re-doing. There's a figure there in the photo that I didn't notice before."

Bert leaned in to take a closer look, staring intently for a few minutes. Claire noticed the slightest hint of alcohol on his breath.

"Actually, that looks a little like the fellow you saw walking down the street the other day. I didn't have a real good look at him, but I think it looks like the same guy. I only saw him from behind, but I recognize the colour of the shirt. Who wears checkered mustard like that?" Claire swallowed the lump in her throat. Musical Director Clara Perova, was at it again, playing the Rockwell's "I've Got a Feeling Somebody's Watching Me" over and over in her head.

Tired of bad news, it suddenly dawned on her how much she really did miss Paul, and how dramatically her life had changed over the past six years. His moving to another country should not make her forget how important he was to her. She felt guilty that they didn't exchange letters as often as they used to. While it was good that she had gained new focus on her life since she began living with Kate, it was definitely time to get back on track with Paul.

His last letter was cheerful and uplifting. He spoke of life in the historic village, and the 19th-century Bakewell tarts and puddings that had now become his passion. Paul said that working in the very bakery where the pastries had originated was motivating, and he felt like he was a part of history. Baking was very different from cooking, he explained. Cooking can be whatever you want it to be, but baking needs to be precise.

Paul gave long descriptions of his walks on the moors of Derbyshire, which sounded magical. These hikes also expanded into the adjacent county of Yorkshire, which was Heathcliff and Catherine country. He saw such visual splendor in every direction, with every turn of his head. His words helped her to create images of the beauty of the landscape and the sounds of sheep everywhere.

He described the neighbouring villages, such as Eyam, home of Britain's last major plague epidemic, where they lost 260 residents to the bubonic plague in 1666. The village had made the heroic decision to self-quarantine but couldn't save everyone. All of the original plague houses were still standing. Paul said walking through the village was like walking back in time. Further along the road towards Sheffield lay Hathersage, a large, busy village with historical and literary associations. Robin Hood's companion, Little John, is buried in the cemetery on the hill. Claire hoped to see all of these places one day.

Without further delay, she put her work aside and settled in to write Paul a long letter. While out of character, she felt it a necessary diversion. She wrote about Ben, Kate, and her work, carefully omitting the current scandal. She told him how she would love to join him and Suki on their long hikes across the moors to see places like Jacob's Ladder and Mam Tor, and she would try to come soon.

It struck her as odd that the same desire wasn't there to speak with her parents. They seemed happy alone, and they were always wrapped up in their own lives. Claire never thought that they made good parents. She and Paul were more of a necessary inconvenience than a passion. Although she had grown closer to them before they moved to the coast, she still resented many things about her childhood. She never hated her parents, but expectations and fundamental disagreements weighed on her since childhood. Then there was the guilt trip that she was away when her grandparents died. They wanted her to come home, and yet they had been noticeably displeased when she returned home without Oliver.

By contrast, her parents had always held a high opinion of Paul. This was in part perhaps because he had moved so far away and was no longer around to be judged. It also probably helped that he was a boy, and boys can do no wrong. Their parents idealized him as the proverbial son. Being a girl was more complicated. Claire had questions and failures, and she quickly became the disappointment. She was unmarried and no saint. Her ambitions and her dreams were tempered with her mother's conservative views. But that was then, this is now.

Claire made a note to go back and re-shoot the estates, and she resolved to be more careful this time. The weatherman was calling for a few days of rain, so she planned to go sooner rather than later. She would enjoy the drive to that side of town, so having to return wasn't a hardship. What was more troubling was the figure in her photos. Could it really have been Wolf? Was he really following her? In her mind, Claire tried to piece together the information she had received thus far. Unfortunately, she didn't have much. Claire still had too many questions, but far too few answers.

Chapter 20

Once settled by a phone, she picked up the message that Ruth had handed her. She read it again while picking up the receiver. She hesitated before she dialed the number. It had to be Will's old neighbour. But why on earth would Maria be calling her?

"Hello, Maria? This is Claire Perova. I am returning your call."

A meek voice answered through the line, "Thank you for calling me back. This might sound a little strange, but I was hoping we could meet somewhere. I know you knew Will. I heard from Glen. I don't know if he told you anything about me, but maybe you can help me."

"Maria, what would Will have told me?" She muttered to herself, *What is this shit?*

"I would prefer if we met in person. Maybe lunch?"

Three days later, at the assigned location, a reluctant Claire sat waiting for her lunch companion. She had left home in a hurry that morning, having spent too much time putting together her equipment for a client that she was meeting afterwards. Looking up at the sky on the way to her car, Claire noticed that it was a gloomy day. She had an equally gloomy feeling about this meeting, although she wasn't sure why.

Unlike Kate, who always needed to look professional on the job, Claire had the luxury of dressing casually. Today, she wore linen slacks and a wrap-around sweater, and she had her hair pulled back in a loose braid. She watched the door. A few minutes later, a very attractive Latina woman walked in. She was well dressed in a floral print dress with matching flats, and her hair was loosely tied up in a bun. She was roughly the same age as Claire.

Maria joined her at her table and ordered a burger and fries. She was eager to talk, and the story that unfolded took Claire completely off guard. Maria was twenty-one when she went to live in Toronto with her friend Elyse, who was just nineteen at the time. Elyse was studying at University, and Maria was working as a Girl Friday for a marketing company. Although they were rather young to be living on their own, they seized the opportunity when it was presented to them.

Elyse had an older cousin, Dany Berra, who had come to Toronto a few years ago to find a new life. But he had fallen into old habits of drugs and petty theft, and he had recently been struggling. He returned to his family in Venezuela, and the plan was to stay for two years to pay off some debts and try to regain his footing. So, rather than lose the apartment, he offered to sublet it to his cousin. It was difficult for Maria's father to allow these youngsters to be on their own, but Maria begged him to give them a chance to try it. Their parents tried to come often, and they called the girls every other day.

Maria had initially taken few things from her home, and once things seemed to be working out well, she asked her father whether he could find the time to bring her remaining belongings. As a favour to Jorge, Will and his neighbor, a German man, offered to drive her things down. Jorge was very grateful, and he helped to load the belongings into Will's truck. That's when Will first met Maria's roommate, Elyse.

Maria wasn't aware of this immediately, but apparently Will had gone down a few times after that to visit Elyse while Maria was at work. Maria came home one day in time to see Will heading toward the parking lot. When Maria confronted Elyse, she was told that Will had seduced her, that he forced himself on her. Elyse was confessing this now, but Maria wondered why she waited so long to tell her. It had now been weeks since Will first started his trips down to see her.

"She was nineteen, and Will was thirty-one years old, with a wife and a four-year-old daughter at home. I screamed at her, 'My God, what were you thinking?' I demanded to know why she hadn't told me sooner. She almost refused to hear me. Was I supposed to blame Will for this? I didn't understand what was going on."

Claire sat patiently listening, still wondering how this would all relate to her, and why Maria was telling her any of it.

"Time passed and a few months later, I saw Will at the apartment again," Maria went on. "I really was furious, and I begged Elyse not to see him anymore. I said that what he was doing was wrong from every possible angle. This is exactly one of the reasons why my father was so concerned for us. But I think Will was giving her money, because we always had lots of good food, the expensive stuff that we couldn't have afforded. And she bought things for the apartment. Still, she told me she would stop and that she would tell Will as much. I don't know if I believed her or not," she said after a considerable pause.

"It was about a month later that Elyse went missing and then her body was found over the Scarborough Bluffs, down on the rocky beach. It was highly unlikely that she would have gone there, or that she just *happened* to fall over the cliff. She had drugs in her system but believe, me she didn't do drugs. The police eventually dropped the case because they had no leads, but I know there was more going on."

"So, you spoke with the police?" asked Claire

"Yes, they came to the apartment a few times after that, and I know they spoke with Elyse's parents many times. But I didn't think they were trying too hard to find out what happened. They simply concluded that Elyse went there with someone and had taken some drugs. They figured that she likely wandered too close to the edge while she was under the influence. And because she was a young immigrant, I fear that nobody was too interested. Hers was simply labeled a death by misadventure."

Claire remembered the Scarborough Bluffs as a ruggedly splendid, but little known area on the edge of the land overlooking Lake Ontario—a fifteen-kilometer stretch of escarpment with trails above, winding down to the beaches below the cliffs. She had only been there once, as it was a well-known spot for daytime hikers, photographers, and tourists. She had taken some panoramic shots of the cliffs, comprised of glacial sediment. She heard that they had recently developed an erosion problem, sometimes with six-metre chunks falling off the cliffs. As a result, people were urged to stay away, particularly at night. As an off-limits area, it drew new crowds.

Aside from gaining notoriety for late-night gang parties, it was becoming known within her University community that some addicts from the nearby area of Cabbagetown would come out to the bluffs at night to party and to shoot up their drugs. Local residents, who moved to the area because of the alluring beauty, now disliked all of the attention the bluffs were receiving.

Claire remembers being surprised when she learned that the community of Cabbagetown got its name from the fact that in the1870s, the Irish immigrants were digging up their front lawns to plant cabbages. Although this had become a somewhat derelict area, it was a popular place for new immigrants because of the affordable housing. Many students preferred to live there because of the proximity to community schools and colleges. Claire knew this area well, as many of her University friends had lived here. On many occasions, she had met fellow students for lunches at one of the many cafes in the area. She and Oliver had often met at a cafe at Carlton and Parliament Streets at the end of the day, when their classes were over. A seedier side of the area was revealed at night, though. Riverdale Park would regularly fill up with junkies after dark.

It was disturbing to think that in the end, Elyse would be categorized as just another unfortunate death at the Bluffs.

Chapter 21

MARIA CONTINUED HER STORY, STILL PICKING AT THE FEW fries that were left on her plate. "Two days later, when Will showed up at the door, I refused to open it, I was convinced that he had killed her, but he was ranting on about having had nothing to do with it. He almost changed my mind. There was something about the way he was talking—the fear in his voice that sounded very real. But still, I wouldn't open the door, and the last thing he said was 'Watch your back.' I have not seen him since. I honestly don't know if that was meant as a warning for me to be careful, or if it was a threat."

"I was afraid to go to the cops about Will, since my family was still awaiting official residence status, and I didn't want to put my parents in a bad predicament. If my father suspected that Will had anything to do with it, he would have killed him, and that would have been very bad for our family. My father would go to jail and we would be sent back to Argentina. How was I to know whether he was threatening me or not? He knows where my family lives, and he could have caused a lot of trouble. I was panicking because of the discovery of drugs in Elyse's body, and that put me under a lot of scrutiny from my family, her family, and the police."

"Did you stay in the apartment after that?"

"Well, I did for a while. But nobody could contact Dany, so eventually I had to move back home. My father came to move my things and we left the apartment empty. Oh how I cried for Elyse."

All Claire could do was sit there and stare at her in incredulity.

Maria went on to speculate, "But the oddest thing had happened, and I didn't notice it until a few days after Will came to the apartment. When Elyse and I would go out, I started noticing two men with red hair. Not big men—but they looked like twins. Maybe it was just a coincidence, but I started seeing them everywhere we went. I'd see them in the coffee shop, they would walk past the restaurant where we ate, and sometimes I'd see them when we were shopping for groceries. I thought there was likely no connection, maybe they had just moved into the neighborhood. But after Elyse died, I did notice that the men were no longer around. They simply vanished from sight."

Maria was unsure whether Will could have inadvertently or purposely led the men to her, so she protected herself under the safety of family. According to Maria, now that Will was dead, she felt a little safer to venture out. Her main concern was to help Elyse's family find some answers. She would feel so much better, and it would help alleviate some guilt—not only for herself, but also for her parents, who were now being shunned by Elyse's family, through no fault of their own. Maria was following the theory that the two men didn't know who she was or where she was from, figuring that otherwise, they would have found her by now.

"This is a lot for me to digest, Maria, I can't believe you

carried this around with you for all these years. But I'm not quite sure why you are telling me all this. Why me, and why now?" This news came down on Claire with such force it was like being hit by a train. "I'm not sure what this has to do with me."

"I was thinking that he is dead and he can't hurt me anymore. So maybe now I could ask you if he told you anything about this. Maybe something that might bring some closure for Elyse's family. Maybe he spoke to you about it. I'm always frightened, and I miss my friend. I thought you might know who those redheaded men are, or whether they are Will's friends." She stared at Claire waiting for an answer. "Did he tell you about them?"

Claire looked at the forgotten piece of bread in her hand. She was in shock. She looked at Maria and said, "I almost wish you didn't tell me this. I don't have any information for you, and I think I was better off not knowing anything that you have told me. I am so sorry, but I can't help you. All of this happened a long time ago, what—about six years now? And it happened in Toronto, which is an entirely different juris-diction." Claire thought for a moment. "Have you contacted the Toronto police now that Will is dead? Did the police ever question Will after Elyse was found?"

Maria smiled faintly and said, "I knew it was a long shot asking you. I just had nowhere else to turn. My concern was how well you knew Will, and how much he told you. I already know what conclusion the police came to back then. I don't think that I will contact them again. What is the saying? 'Let sleeping dogs lie.'"

Claire's pager started ringing. She had completely lost track of time. She told Maria that she had to go, as she was late for a rendezvous with some sellers. She awkwardly said goodbye to this woman and left the restaurant. Claire was mindful of the way her legs shook as she walked. It was pouring rain, and she would look a mess by the time she reached her car. Could this day possibly get any worse? She felt herself being pulled into an abyss of fear, sadness, rage, and helplessness. At each turn, she was learning things about this man that she didn't want to know. Bruce Springsteen's "Brilliant Disguise" came to Clara Perova's musical genius mind.

How could she have been so wrong about him? She wasn't bothered that he slept with other women, but that it was *these* women in particular. One was not much more than a child, the other a married woman. If you put a picture next to the definition of immoral, that would be it. He was a sleazy scumbag, plain and simple. She felt humiliated and cheap. Claire had never felt disrespected before, and it sickened her to feel this way.

The added possibly of him being a murderer distressed her to say the least. His talk of loving animals and nature sounded hypocritical and disingenuous. How about his disregard of humans? When she pictured him, his smile became a little less appealing. Just the thought of his hands on her body, his breath on her face had become something offensive and smutty.

And that nagging doubt—*did he kill Elyse*? Why were "watch your back" his last words to Maria? Claire hadn't been there to hear the words so didn't know how to interpret them. She couldn't decide if it was a protective warning or a personal threat. She also made a mental note that Maria's story didn't quite make sense to her, and she hadn't answered any of her own questions. Why did it matter so much to Maria what Will had told her? She had strong misgivings about Maria, and she was sure that sooner or later, she would figure out what it was about the conversation that bothered her. It left her with a bad taste in her mouth.

Chapter 22

Claire called, "Good morning Ruth," as she entered the office. It had taken Claire a long time to refer to this woman as "Ruth," because she had grown up calling her Mrs. Birch. Ruth was the mother of Claire's grade school best friend, Tracey. She remembered all of the sleepovers with warmth, including the giggles that lasted well into the night, until Mrs. Birch would come in and scold them into silence. This woman was the quintessential mother—hugging them warmly, sharing laughter and homemade cookies. Mrs. Birch was the one who always drove them to the skating arena in the winter and to the local pool in the summer.

Claire and Tracey had remained friends right through high school, although her encounters with Mrs. Birch diminished over the years. So, when Claire had started using this office space, it was a pleasant surprise to find Mrs. Birch still working there. Claire had fond memories of Mrs. Birch in this office, , as she and Tracey would often stop in on their way home. So, upon the woman's insistence, she was now "Ruth."

Claire and Tracey stayed in touch as adults. After graduating, Tracey married Bob (formerly known as Bobby in Grade 6), and Claire stood up as maid of honour at their wedding.

Over the years, they made a point of staying in touch, meeting occasionally for a dinner together. That became more difficult after the birth of Tracey's third child, but it was good to hear her news through Ruth. The children were growing like weeds, and they were all in school now. Tracey would love to hear from Claire one day, when she had the time. Another thing that Claire really should do!

Claire's workday was uneventful, and the week ended with a much-anticipated dinner get-together with Kate. They met at their favourite Moroccan restaurant in the heart of the town. Claire was close enough to walk there from her office, so she had stayed behind purposely to avoid an extra trip home. As she walked, she was deciding just how much information she was prepared to heap onto her friend. Once inside the restaurant, she spotted Kate seated near the back, at a cozy table for two.

She was beaming from ear to ear as Claire approached the table. Wine was poured and the menu was perused. For Kate, it was aromatic lamb tagine with dates and for Claire, the spiced fish with ginger. For appetizers, they had roasted cauliflower and kofta. Just reading the menu made Claire's mouth water. One of Claire's greatest pleasures was meal preparation. Even if she was aiming for simple, her dishes somehow ended up being elaborate. Her senses came alive with spices, oils, and the smell of grilling. By a happy coincidence, her favourite place to shop for ingredients was the very store where Paul had worked while she was in Greece. It made her feel connected to him. And he was right when he spoke of the offerings available there. They had a wide range of ethnic and local delicacies that were not available everywhere. Just the smell of a good meal made her want to go home and cook.

Once they had ordered the meal, Kate sat back and casually announced, "I met someone."

"What? When?" Claire was overjoyed at the news. The relevance of something good happening was immense for Claire."

"I met him a while ago, at the Courthouse on my last reporting hearing. His name is Philippe Aldridge. He's a Liaison Officer for the RCMP, and he has just returned from a posting in Panama. He deals with Canadian criminal investigations that are linked to foreign countries, and he has been involved with murder, drug and money laundering cases in Panama. He has just settled here, looking for a less adventurous job at home. He's an awesomely clever guy, Claire. I had noticed him before, but the possibility of us being introduced seemed next to impossible. Then, when I was looking the other way, it suddenly happened. I didn't want to say anything until I was sure, but we've met a few times now, and I'm feeling very positive."

Despite her thoughts being elsewhere, she could not hide her joy at this news. This was coming from a woman who had vehemently sworn off relationships. It was bringing some normalcy back to her world, something that seemed long forgotten. Although Kate wouldn't admit it, her divorce had taken its toll, and Claire could often see the small pieces of her that were missing.

Like her siblings, Kate had desperately wanted children, and although Peter had agreed when they were first married, he had somehow changed his mind almost overnight. The focus was always baseball, hotrods, and the boys. Then, it became late nights and beer, as if he was avoiding the conversation and validating her suspicions through his actions. Once Kate realized that he wouldn't change, she withdrew, and she virtually became invisible to him as he spent less and less time at home. Kate suspected there might have been more than boys and beers during his long absences. She received little sympathy from her mother and father, as they were against the union from the beginning.

"Well, as soon as you have had time to break the ice and get to know one another, I'd love to meet this Philippe," Claire kindly added. Once she had removed her shoes under the table and taken that first sip of her wine, Claire realized she was immensely enjoying this evening. She smiled at the woman sitting across from her. Gone was the frightened new bride who was so desperate to start a new family.

There was something spirited and brilliant about Kate today. She was chatting on with a new energy, about her work at the Notary office and changes she would consider making.

"Maybe it would be in my best interest if I give up the reporting. Being with the right people means everything. It *is* everything. And how fortunate that we are to be able to find that for ourselves, because not everyone can. I am looking forward to when you and Ben can meet him. How exquisitely perfect!"

Kate gushed, "So enough about me, how are you, Claire? It seems like ages since we've sat down together, and I feel like I haven't been here enough for you. I'm sure you have noticed that my mind has been elsewhere."

Although Claire knew that it had only been a few days, it sometimes did feel like forever. They would come and go on different schedules, sometimes leaving each other notes, other times leaving a plate of leftover dinner in the fridge. Having been somewhat inaccessible herself, she was honestly too preoccupied to notice that Kate's mind had also been somewhere else.

With a furrowed brow, Kate went on to say, "I have been so worried about you. Onward and upward, right Claire? I

sincerely hope you have been able let all of this Will stuff go."
Kate never liked Will, and she had no qualms about making it
evident. Claire understood that the news of his death had not
greatly impacted her friend, and Kate's only concern had been
the impact that it had on Claire.

"That's why I love you Kate, you remind me that I'm
flawed," she said with a hearty laugh.

But Claire was suddenly struck with the realization that
'onward and upward' were exactly the opposite in describing how
she felt these past few months. She felt older and more cynical
than she ever could have imagined. She couldn't remember the
last time she had a good laugh. Kate, on the other hand, looked
like the embodiment of youth and optimism. Claire felt very
aware of how unzipped she was. She really did need to get a grip.

"Oh my God, look how early it is," Kate squealed. "Let's
get drunk."

Claire decided that any discussion about Will or Maria or
Bonnie could wait. There was a nagging feeling at the back of her
mind that she couldn't shake, and she wanted to try to make sense
of it before discussing it with Kate. Why did Maria come to see
her? There was no logic to it. Claire suspected the girl was digging
for something she thought Claire knew. It would actually be in
Claire's best interest to dismiss this whole business completely.
Forever. The problem was, at this point she just didn't know how
to go about it. She knew from experience that once her mind took
over, she needed to run with it until her smarter self was able to
regain control. This wasn't happening yet. And besides, this was
Kate's night, and everything else could wait.

Kate was born into a long line of upstanding and dignified
people. As would be expected, this invariably led to assurances

and successes. People in her family were raised well, and they all married well. In a family where optimism reigned, Kate took it as a real failure that she married poorly, even though it was her only failure. She had been given opportunities for a good education and had used those opportunities well. She and her siblings had always been kind to one another, and she spent a lot of time with her nieces and nephews. She was a good person to have on your side. Her sanguineness and confidence were driven by the fact that it only mattered to her how she viewed herself, and not how others viewed her.

The same wasn't true of Claire, who was raised to worry about what other people thought. Claire and Kate were equipped with differing qualities based on their life experiences, but these differences enhanced them as friends. Claire's family was made up of immigrants, who had lost everything and needed to start over. It wasn't easy to learn how to be poor in a new country. It was quite reasonable for them to worry and to have a certain level of distrust and caution. Living with Kate helped Claire make sense of things, and it kept her levelled. She had become a shining example of optimism, and lately Claire had taken to comparing her actions to "what would Kate have done."

Take the time she was trying to write a speech for Paul's wedding, for instance. She had left a notepad and pen by her bedside and during the night if inspiration struck, she would jot down notes. That night she was rife with good ideas and scribbled her notes in the dark, but when morning came, she realized that there was no ink in her pen. Kate would have checked the pen the night before.

"Yes, maybe," laughed Kate. "But I wouldn't have bothered to wake up to write a single thing."

Chapter 23

ON THIS CLEAR TUESDAY MORNING, CLAIRE RETURNED once again to Rocky Ridge Estates. This time, she carefully checked her subject areas to ensure that there was no sign of people lingering about. On a good note, being a different time of day, the lighting was far better. It was a still day, without the slightest hint of a breeze. She was sure these shots would be an improvement from the previous ones. Claire smelled the air and let out a relaxing sigh. The cool nights had caused the leaves to keep turning, so the colours were more vibrant, more pronounced, and this pleased her.

Using her tripod, Claire's goal was to create a spherical shot with distorted edges for the cover of the brochure. She planned on using leading lines and a lot of sky. This was a good opportunity to try a few tricks she had learned in University, as this setting provided very good landscaping and architecture. Her degree in photography didn't happen, but it was time that she start using some of the techniques she had learned. After a few satisfying hours, she headed back to her car to pack away her things.

Just as she started the engine, a car pulled up in front of her. As the figure exited his car, she realized who it was: Wolf! Her first reaction was panic, but there was something about his body language that made her breathe easy. It was not a bad thing to be confronted by this person at last. With a healthy intake of air, she rolled down her window.

The man approaching her walked with an easy gait, lilting slightly to one side. He was likely somewhere in his late fifties, sporting a thick mop of greying hair and a pair of spectacles that sat halfway down his nose. While still experiencing mild anxiety, something about him definitely suggested that she was not in any danger. He moved slowly and calmly, and he made a waving gesture in greeting her.

"I need to have a word miss," he spoke softly, with a thick German accent when she opened her window to accommodate him. Although all of Claire's previous perceptions of Wolf had been threatening, he was now coming across as a very gentle man.

"I'm sorry for approaching you like this," he uttered apologetically. "My name is Wolfgang Krueger, but I think you know who I am, because you seem to be following me."

Claire shut off her engine.

"I know who you are, and I have seen you so many times, Mr. Krueger. But why have *you* been watching *me*? It seems to me that it's you who is following me, not the other way around. I saw you at the memorial service where you were definitely watching me, and again by my office."

Wolf raised his eyebrows as he pondered what she had just said.

"I don't know where your office is. But I do know you were Will's friend and had been visiting him. But after he died, why is it that you were here taking pictures of me? Is that why you are here today?"

Seeing the confusion on her face, he added, "I do work

here. I was on that flat right over there, behind the Estates, checking out some specs for the builder, and you drove up near where we are now, through the main gate. I saw you with your camera, and you were photographing me. And I think it was you watching me at Will's memorial service. Can you please tell me what your interest in me is?"

"I am here working for the developer also, as I was when I accidentally photographed you. I'm taking some promotional shots for sales brochures. I had no idea you were standing there! I'm actually here to do retakes because my shots were ruined."

Wolf hesitated before continuing. "It seems we have some confusion."

"It's like the Donovan song, 'Season of the Witch,'" she accidentally said out loud.

"Which what?" asked Wolf.

"When I look over my shoulder, I see some other cat looking over his shoulder at me," she explained.

"I don't understand."

"I'm sorry, forget it. It's just a song."

He stood up and looked around, as though deep in thought. He leaned back down towards her open window. "I know of a little luncheon down the road, simple but quite good. Can I buy you a sandwich?" he smiled warmly. "I haven't eaten all day."

Claire followed his car down the street to the cafe. She was dumbfounded that humans could be so predisposed to make snap character judgements, based on anything but fact. What a human flaw! She was looking forward to this encounter, which somehow was very timely.

Chapter 24

WOLF LED HER UP THE LIGHT-FILLED STAIRCASE, TO AN upper alcove where they could talk privately. The room wasn't large, but it was brightly lit and extremely welcoming. The charming ambience was enhanced by enticing smells coming from the kitchen. Claire had driven by this place many times over the years, but she had never been inside, and coming here made her wonder why she hadn't. The exterior of the bistro was adorned with worn-out clapboard that may have been white once, but was now chipped, peeling, and heavily covered with ivy. She found the place somehow enchanting, which added to her comfort. Following a friendly exchange with the waitress, they both ordered Reuben sandwiches with a mug of beer for Wolf, a glass of wine for Claire.

"When I first immigrated to Canada from Germany, it took me a long time to miss German food. I was more interested in the wide range of choices here. But now, I can enjoy it again," offered Wolf.

"Can I ask how long you have been here in Canada, Mr. Krueger?" replied Claire. She felt comfortable with this big man. His expressive eyes with their generous lids somehow gave him the appearance of a hound dog.

"Please, call me Wolf. I came in 1952, when I was 20 years old. That's the same year that Volkswagen came to Canada, what do you think of that?" He laughed. "I imagine you were not even born then," teased Wolf.

"Actually, I was one."

"Well, you don't look old enough to have been born then." He smiled kindly before continuing, "I wrote a letter to my father's best friend, who lived in Canada, asking if I could come to him to refine my trade and start a life for myself. He did permit me to come, and I lived in his home for four years, until he received word that his niece was also planning to come live with him. By then, I had saved some money, and with some help from my father and the bank, I was able to buy my own house. I was there the day his niece arrived, and I think I fell in love with her instantly as she stepped off the bus. I felt it almost right away, that she was my *seelenverwandte*. My soulmate. We did eventually marry, and now we have the life that we both wanted. Those are Ilsa's horses at our home. She is quite a competent rider, not so much me. Actually, you are not unlike her in many ways. I think you would like each other."

She smiled at the compliment—the second smile that Wolf had drawn out of her so far.

"When Will came to live at the house next door, we became quite simpatico. He was a likeable fellow, and he was always there to lend a hand if anything broke down. We have had many pleasurable chats over the back fence, and we shared many beers. It was difficult for Will when his mother passed, and aside from his partner, Glen, he didn't seem to have many friends. But I was a good neighbour and friend to him, and we grew to like one another."

Wolf spoke slowly and with precision, as if it were important to get the story right.

"Will gave the impression of having done very well for himself," he continued between bites of his sandwich. "I don't know how much money a man can make in his business, and I expect that his mother may have had a small sum to leave him, but still. He seemed to have prospered very well. I also noticed that he had a lot of time to himself and was not always at work. It was Glen who always seemed overworked and handled the bulk of the car repairs. I also noticed that there was frequently a car at his cottage, and it would stay for long periods of time. I wouldn't ask who the woman was, and he didn't offer to tell me. When Will asked me if I had some time to help move a few items to Toronto as a favour for his old neighbor Jorge, I didn't hesitate to lend a hand. This was not a big task, and I enjoyed the idea of driving to Toronto, as we don't go there often. This was quite some time ago, and I had more strength back then," he laughed.

Wolf took a drink of his beer before continuing. "During this trip, I met this Maria girl, at her apartment in Toronto. And that was the day Will and I met her friend Elyse, an alluring girl that seemed much older than her years. When I say alluring, I don't necessarily mean charming. More like a spider luring someone to her web. When I first came from Germany at twenty, I had met girls like her. I didn't care for this Elyse. She was definitely all 'come hither' with Will. Actually, I didn't much care for the other one either. I think both of those girls had eyes for him. It seemed like they were competing for his attention, as I could see fire in that Maria's eyes. It was not a good situation."

Claire squirmed in her seat as she listened to how much

this story differed from Maria's.

Wolf reflected out loud, "I think that girl was headed down the wrong path and Will would have followed the bread-crumbs. But unfortunately, Will loved her attention. I know he went back there on more than one occasion. My opinion of him changed overnight. I became annoyed with him for even entertaining the thought of going near that young girl. Personally, I would not have been surprised to hear that this was her occupation."

As Clare listened to Wolf's story, things started falling into place. All of this explained Will's comments about not wanting to speak with Wolf. It must have been for this reason that he and Will had a falling out of sorts and had not spoken in years. Claire was touched by Wolf's benevolent demeanor and she realized that it must have been very hard for him to watch Will's actions over the years.

"Will started to act strangely after that, always suspicious. He stayed indoors more, and our conversations slowed down. They didn't stop completely, but they were not as they once were."

"I'm sorry Wolf, I can tell that was hard for you."

"Yes, I suppose it was difficult to lose him as a friend. But Claire, this brings me to the reason why I want to speak with you now. I was there the night that Will died. I was outside with the horses when I saw Will come running out of his house, running away from a car that had driven up his lane. He looked panicked as he crouched around to the far side of the pond where the brambles grow. Then two men got out of the car, and he turned fast. He must have slipped and fell into the water. And I'm sure I heard him hit his head. There was a thud, and then he moaned"

Wolf was no longer eating. "I looked at him, feeling powerless as the men ran over towards the pond. There wasn't much light, but there was enough to make out what was happening. These men looked like they could be twins, they had a remarkable similarity. What I really noticed was their matching haircuts, and the hair colour that was rusty, like red almost. Then, I remembered Will mentioning something about redheaded men around the time that girl was murdered in Toronto. He didn't come right out and say so, but his words suggested that they might have been connected to her death. These had to be them, since one doesn't often see twin men with red hair. They stood there watching like a pair of baboons, with no attempt to help Will out of the water. They ran off when Will stopped moving, like they has just seen a ghost. I don't know if they ran because they had seen me or because Will stopped moving. Also, I had no idea whether they knew who I was, but something told me to be afraid because of the connection to the Toronto girl."

Wolf became animated and his eyes opened wide as he spoke.

"I was afraid to show myself. Everything happened so fast, and I couldn't quite grasp what was going on. If their intentions were bad, as they seemed to be, I could have gotten hurt. I quickly ran back towards the house and hollered for Ilsa to call 911. I then ran back towards the pond, and I climbed over the fence. I had a hard time climbing. It's not a very good fence, and I fell on my leg. I hurt myself pretty badly and that's why I am still limping. I rushed over to where Will was, and I tried to drag him out of the water. Then I slipped and fell on the rocks, hurting the same leg again. He's a big man like me, and dragging his wet body was impossible. So, I just sat in the pond with him, holding his head out of the water until the police and ambulance came. It was completely dark by then. The way I was sitting, half in and half out of the water, I couldn't try any CPR, not that I would know what I was doing anyway. The paramedics took him out of the water, but I think he was already dead."

Wolf stopped talking and Claire was worried that he wasn't going to say anything else.

"What happened then?" she coaxed.

"Once the ambulance took him away, the police drove me back to my house, so I could change into dry clothes and give them my statement. I told them everything except the part about the men."

"Why didn't you tell them, Wolf?"

"Something about them was disturbing, and it was clear that Will was very frightened by them. He saw those men in Toronto when Elyse died and if he thought they were involved, maybe they were coming for him as well. I still don't know if they saw me. Maybe they ran because they didn't know what else to do. But I was worried that if I said anything, they would come to hurt my Ilsa. Afterwards, Ilsa drove me to the hospital to have my leg checked out. I bruised my femur and tore some ligaments but fortunately, I didn't do any major damage."

Wolf rubbed his leg in a way that suggested that he was feeling the pain all over again. "I am now afraid that people are following me, including you," he began again. "I even started to think that you might be connected to them, and that you were watching me for that reason. That's how crazy the mind can be. I was uncertain what to tell the police because although they hadn't killed Will, that might have been their plan. But if their intent was injurious in nature, Ilsa thought it best if I said nothing. We want no trouble with these people. They know where I live, and it would be obvious that I was the one who spoke out."

With a pointing finger and a fatherly tone, he added, "I need you to be careful. You may find out something you don't want to know. By asking too much, you may be alerting people of your curiosity and any new knowledge that you acquire. And you could be placing yourself in harm's way! I have no idea what they wanted with Will. What did he get himself into? There may be a real danger if they had anything to do with that girl's murder."

They ended their lunch with a heartfelt goodbye, both feeling grateful for having met. As Wolf walked her to her car, he added, "I hope that their business with Will is concluded, and that they need nothing more to do with me. I still struggle about whether to call police because I don't know if it would be dangerous. But I think that you need to be prudent, and don't get too close to the situation."

They spent the next few minutes exchanging contact information, each expressing the desire to stay in touch. Claire was very drawn to this gentle soul of a man, and she hoped that she would have the chance to see him again.

Chapter 25

CLAIRE DROVE AWAY, WONDERING IF SHE SHOULD HAVE told Wolf about the conversation she had with Maria two days earlier. She was bothered by how much Maria's version differed from Wolf's. Was Will and Elyse's relationship mutual, as told by Wolf? Or had Will seduced and possibly raped her, as told by Maria? Strangely, the two men with red hair showed up in both accounts. There was a very real possibility that the men had connected Will to Elyse. They had either killed the girl and then wanted to kill Will for reasons unknown to Claire, or they knew that Will had killed Elyse and were seeking revenge. Claire didn't want to frighten Wolf, but she told herself that if it became necessary, she could go and see him again.

Claire was also becoming increasingly curious about Daniela. Was she the woman Wolf had seen at the cottage? Would those men be after her as well? Were they interested in a connection between Daniela and Will? Claire could not just sit back and do nothing. She remembered something Wolf had said to her. "Wasn't it Albert Einstein who said, 'The world is a dangerous place to live, not because of the people who are evil, but because of the people who don't do anything about it?'"

With so much running around in her head, Claire's

concentration was not on her driving. Rounding the bend, she almost ran into three emergency vehicles that were pulled over. Nearby, a tow truck was pulling a badly mangled car out of the ditch. As she slowed down, she couldn't help but look over. The car seemed to have hit a tree, and the tow truck had turned it upright. At this moment, emergency workers were in the progress of removing the body from the wreckage. No indication how many passengers or their status. She grabbed the wheel more tightly for the rest of the journey home with a sick feeling in the pit of her stomach. Now was not the time to have her mind anywhere else but on the road.

This seemed like an unusual place for an accident to occur, since the road was relatively straight, and there was very little traffic at this time of day. Could the driver have experienced some duress that caused the car to career out of control? The scene had fortunately attracted very little attention, so there was no traffic backup. Claire was grateful that there was no delay in getting home.

Entering their modest front hall, she walked through the house calling Kate's name. It was a hot day and the breeze was gently blowing the curtains through the open windows. Claire eventually found her out back, in their vegetable garden.

From the deck, Claire called, "Hey there, little miss green thumb!" She stepped down onto the grass and was instantly aware of how long it was. Maybe it was her turn to cut it this week?

"Looks like it's harvesting time. Do you need any help?" she said as she approached the spot where Kate was kneeling. "Looks like we have some decent produce for the next little while," commented Claire as she admired the tomatoes, carrots, and potatoes in Kate's basket."

Watching Kate was a wonderful reminder of her own childhood. Claire had such fond memories of her grandmother's garden when she was still alive. Claire's grandparents had come over from Russia with her parents after the Second World War. They were among the millions of displaced people who ended up in Germany after the war, either from opposing Stalin or being placed in forced labour camps. Originally, her grandparents and their relatives had lived in small collective communities before being driven out by the German troops during the war.

Claire's grandparents and parents fled their homes, families, and friends, now separated forever amidst the turmoil. All were eventually captured and herded into refugee camps somewhere in central Germany, and they remained there for years, until the war ended. The detainees in these camps were later liberated by the American troops, and they were given the opportunity to immigrate to Canada. Weeks after arriving in Toronto, Claire was born.

Claire's grandmother meant the world to her. After having lost so much in the old country, the woman fervently loved what remained of her family. Family was what was most important. *Samoye Glavnoye*. Claire loved her dearly, and her passing had a real impact on her. Her fondest memories of her and Paul's weekend visits were of her grandmother carrying her and her brother up to bed, one on each arm, after they had fallen asleep watching a Disney movie.

The woman was humble to a fault, and she stressed the importance of being so. Her hands were rough and her clothing was worn, but she hummed all day as she went about her chores. Loyalty and strength were foremost, and the woman never complained—it must have been good old Russian stoicism. She represented stability and fidelity, and Claire learned the value of rules from her. But her grandmother trusted few, and it was important to her that the family did nothing to draw attention to themselves. And it was equally important that her family always presented well. If the clothes weren't clean, or the laughs were too loud, she would turn on you.

"Have you no shame?" she would whisper. *U tebye net styda?*

But what Claire loved best was her gentleness, her laughter, and her large, doting hugs. There was such sadness in this woman's eyes, and her love of the old country was apparent. Claire couldn't even imagine what it would be like to be taken away from everything that she held dear, never to return. But her grandmother was a strong woman who would always adjusted and moved forward, storing away all of the memories of the horrors and death she witnessed. She would forever be vibrant in Claire's memories, this little woman in her patterned dresses, kerchief, and apron. And, of course, memories of the vegetable garden were front and foremost. Claire would sit on the edge of the garden watching in amazement as her grandmother prepared the soil and meticulously and patiently sowed each row.

It was at this time of year that she would run home from school to help with the gathering of her produce. Aside from occasional times that her grandmother would walk her carefully up and down the rows to see the plants in bloom, and later to see the small vegetables beginning to grow, the harvest was the only time she was permitted to step among the plants.

When Paul was very young, Claire was permitted to take him into the garden once everything had been harvested, and they would be free to dig through the remnants for any leftover vegetable scraps. These little bits would then be used in their own bucket of muddy homemade stew. They both wanted to cook like their parents. While mother cooked well, it was more of a necessity, whereas her father had a more passionate approach to his dishes. Claire had good memories of helping dad, fetching things from the cupboard, and standing on a chair beside Paul, watching the pot as he made his famous chicken stew.

On other occasions, Claire would chase butterflies around their yard while her grandparents read under a tree in the shade. As she grew older, she would sit by their feet as, in Russian, they recalled stories from back home. The ones that kept her on the edge of her seat were of their lives before the war began, the ones about gardens, horses, and life on their farm. Claire's grandmother grew up in a southern part of Russia, near the Black Sea. Little did she know she would never again see her beloved *Chernoye More*. They lost their land to Stalin, and they were instead set up in collective farms, or *kolkhoz*. Nearly a million of the wealthiest farmers were removed from their land, and they were never seen again. In the end, none of this mattered to Claire's family, as the war eventually took them away from their homes. For them, being free in Canada, with a garden of their own, meant a lot.

Claire's grandfather would recall stories of the horrors of war, of the bloodshed, the loss, and the tears. Relatives were seen hanging in the town square, their crimes unknown. He talked of the fear they felt when they heard the air raids and the planes coming. They would huddle, cover their ears, and pray that they were not today's target. How they ached to go home! But once released from the camps, going home was no longer an option. Those returning would find themselves on trains headed for Siberia and most likely to death camps, courtesy of Stalin.

At the time, Claire was much too young to fully grasp the magnitude of the horrors they were describing to her. She would give anything to be able to hug them both now and say, "I get it now." *Teper ya ponimayu.*

Kate interrupted her thoughts. "I was thinking that we should go downtown overnight. Let's have some dinner, drink too much wine, and maybe go and see a movie? How about "Dirty Dancing?" I see it just came out this week. It's Patrick Swayze, Claire. And it seems the opportune time to go – maybe our last chance before the weather starts to cool off. Phillip is away this week, so the timing is good for me. You and I used to go to the movies often, but I don't think we've been down once this summer."

The thought of going away right now was not exactly at the top of her to-do list, but Claire acquiesced, nonetheless. She went upstairs to call Ben, telling him about her plans to be away and promising to see him in two days. The sound of his encouraging voice calmed her, and she hung up the phone feeling more collected about a spontaneous getaway. With a smile, she changed her clothes, tied back her hair, and washed her face and hands before returning to the kitchen to grill some fish for dinner.

She set aside some fresh herbs, olives, and, feta. Paired with Kate's fresh tomatoes, this meal would be heavenly.

"Good food and good music. Is there a better way to soothe my soul? Yes, I believe a glass of wine would certainly help."

Kate came in the back door with her bushel of deliciousness. Brushing the perspiration from her brow, she called into the kitchen.

"Hey, are you talking to yourself again? Oh, and by the way," she hollered into the kitchen, "it's your turn to cut the grass."

Chapter 26

Claire and Kate cleared their work schedules and met at home early in the afternoon. They packed a few things and headed out to Kate's car. Claire settled comfortably into the passenger seat. It would take no longer than an hour to drive into Toronto. Kate had called the night before and booked them into a place near the movie theatre and restaurants. Claire used the time to lean her head back and close her eyes, enjoying the motion of the car and the warmth of the sun on her face. The radio was on, and it didn't take her long to doze off. Kate was excited to be away for the night and smiled over at her sleeping friend.

After checking in to the Hazleton Hotel on Yorkville Avenue, they decided to explore the area while finding a place to eat. It was a balmy evening and they appreciated the coolness offered by the shade of the buildings. They first wandered through the heart of Yorkville, down Cumberland Avenue, and finally settled on a steak house on Scollard Street. Although a far cry from how it looked in the seventies, there were still plenty of reminders of the popularity of Yorkville..

Back in the late sixties, Yorkville exploded onto the scene with its smoky coffee houses, hippie boutiques, and creative talent, ranging from readings by the up and coming Margaret

Atwood to musical performances from every genre. Many referred to the area as Toronto's Haight-Ashbury. One could see go-go dancers in their glass cubes at the Mynah Bird, while listening to their favourite house bands, or hang out at The Mousehole to see good bands like The Checkmates, The Mandala, and Gordon Lightfoot, to name a few. Overall, Claire had known little about the area during her university days and had only visited a few times. She and Oliver had embarked on their Greek experience, so she missed a lot of the action, but she remembered how they sat in blow-up chairs at The Riverboat and saw one of Joni Mitchell's first concerts.

The area was much different now, being mostly high-end stores and residential living. It was a complete turnaround from the vibrant community it once was. Back then, it felt more pedestrian, with bricked streets, hanging baskets, and outdoor cafes. Claire also remembered that Tony's nightclub, the Cabana was around here somewhere, but she decided not to bring it up in conversation.

Claire and Kate ordered their meal, suddenly feeling very hungry. For starters, they decided to share the escargots bourguignon, with a bottle of chianti. They each ordered a medium rare steak with tiger prawns. Enjoying the wine and the appetizer, they soon realized that the movie wasn't going to happen. They had yet to receive their main course. They were so engrossed in their evening that to interrupt it with a movie would be sacrilegious, even though they had travelled all this way to go the theatre. Patrick Swayze would have to wait.

The waiter came and refilled their glasses, and before long, the conversation turned to Will. Claire filled Kate in on what she knew.

"Will's likely not evil, he's just an idiot," Kate commented. "A bonehead. And I don't think he deserved to die just for that. What I don't understand is this: did those men mean to *kill* him, or just to shake him up a bit?"

"What really bothers me, Kate, is that he was well aware of his actions and of the potential consequences, yet he carried on. Then, when confronted, he ran like a coward. So, he's not only a degenerate and a two-timer, but he's also spineless. And a liar, and maybe a murderer!" Kate looked at her in silence, unaccustomed to such outbursts from Claire.

Following a brief discussion, the friends decided to pay their bill and take the conversation back to the hotel room, where they could get comfortable and curl up in their beds. Once settled into pajamas and curled up in bed, Claire mused, "Why would the same men be seen at two different crime scenes? I know there has to be some connection, but I can't see one."

"I know you think that, but what if Elyse had a whole other thing going on?" Kate was fully engaged in this conversation. She took another sip of her wine. "What do you say we finish this bottle and solve your mystery by morning?" Claire rolled her eyes but didn't turn the refill down. "Didn't you say she was living in her cousin's apartment?" continued Kate excitedly. "And didn't you say that he was back in Venezuela somewhere? Maybe he was tangled up in something that Elyse didn't even know about. And how does Maria fit into all of this? She just moves home as if nothing has happened? Maybe it really *was* drug-related or something! And maybe Will also became a target because he was seen with her. These guys saw the two of them coming out of what's-his-name's apartment, and bingo! They were suddenly tangled up in it, poor suckers."

Kate seemed deep in thought. Then, she suddenly looked up at Claire and said, "or maybe those men weren't after the girl at all! Maybe they just wanted to get her away from Will? Maybe her cousin sent them. Or Daniela!"

Claire smiled at her friend's approach to things, yet she was stunned at the things she was saying.

"Whoa there girl, now you are worse than me! Don't get carried away here. Who's being Nancy Drew now?" She grabbed a chip from the bowl.

"Okay Kate, but what about Daniela? Didn't she threaten to break Will's legs if he tried to break up with her? Although don't people always say things like that? How many times in a fit of anger did one of us mutter, "I'm going to kill you?""

They looked at each other with a kind of tragic humour. "So, now we are getting way off track. She would have nothing to do with those guys. It might be some other thing that Will did, or something else he knew." Kate picked at her fingernail before adding, "And I thought Michael Jackson buying the Elephant Man's bones was weird."

They hypothesized into the wee hours and finally decided to call it a night. Oddly enough, Claire found the sound of the city traffic soothing, and she didn't stay awake for very long. Claire's sleep was troubled and fitful, but still she woke up feeling rested.

The following morning, they decided to go for a long walk to the waterfront before heading home. It was a fabulously clear and sunny day, with just a hint of a breeze. Whether or not they had solved anything last night, her head did feel clearer, if not just for this opportunity to get things off her chest. While she had been against this overnight trip, she realized it had been a good idea.

They passed a restaurant that was undergoing renovations, and the workers were carrying in sheets of plywood and cans of paint. Somewhere at the back of the restaurant, the hammering was starting. Claire recognized that they were speaking Greek and in the background, she could make out Cretan folk music. She didn't know whether to laugh or cry.

"Does it still bother you a lot?" asked Kate.

"Well, like John Cougar said, "It Hurts so Good." That's likely the best way to explain it. What I miss the most is not the places I visited, but more the people that I met along the way. Those are my most vivid memories. I left friendships, not to mention all of my photographs and undeveloped rolls of film. And oddly enough, I miss my shawl. I had this blue crochet shawl that I would wear in the evenings. Its funny I would remember that."

They had reached the water by now, and the sounds instantly changed to screaming gulls and roaring boat engines. For Claire, there were few things more exhilarating than the smell of the open water. She stood in the dappled shade of the trees, closed her eye, and breathed. They slowed their walk.

"Did I ever tell you about the time when I was working in Sfakia that I decided to go for a walk? The road along the coast had always appealed to me, and I had never gone in that direction, so on this day, when I finished at noon, I decided to walk along the coast to see where it went. I knew the town of Matala was about forty kilometres down the road in the same direction. Do you know that Joni Mitchell song, "Carrie"? She had written it about her experiences while living there. I felt a connection and thought it would have been exciting if I had run into her there. Anyway, after an hour of walking along this hot, very dusty road, I realized that I was going nowhere in a hurry. Then I lost track of how long I had been walking. It was so hot, and I was very thirsty. I finally turned back, as I'm sure my stubbornness made me walk further than my common sense would have normally allowed.

I realized that I had gone too far, and there was a moment of panic because I thought I would die of heat stroke and thirst. As I headed back, I also noticed the lack of cars on the road. No cars, no people, and not even the sound of sheep or goats on the hillsides. Each of those sounds were usually omnipresent, so I was aware of the quiet. Just when I was beginning to worry, I saw a thin line of dust weaving along the coast from behind. On each bend, the dust was getting closer and closer. I turned around and began waving both my arms frantically hoping the car would stop for me.

It was a taxicab, and in the rear was one passenger, a girl about my age. She motioned for the driver to stop. Rolling down her window, she asked me where I was going. She was going back to Chania and agreed to drop me in Sfakia, so I climbed in the back beside her. It started out with 'Oh are you American?' 'No, I'm from Canada,' 'Oh, so am I!' Then we realized that we both came from the same town. Then, turns out that she was from my neighborhood and went to senior high with Paul. We started laughing and screaming, and the driver almost threw us out of the cab because he thought we were fighting. It was brilliant! Tell me, what are the odds of that happening?"

Still laughing, Claire added, "I have often wondered if that is written somewhere in the Encyclopedia of Superstitions and if it holds any specific meaning?"

"Maybe it just meant that you would get home safely," suggested Kate.

Chapter 27

CLAIRE GOT UP AND FINISHED HER TEA. "BEN, I REALLY have to go. As hard as it is to leave, we both need to be somewhere else."

Ben had called Claire early to say that he was working from home this morning and had the time to come over for a quick visit. He could do this now that Adam was in school full time. It was already Wednesday. Wasn't it just Wednesday? The days were going by far too quickly. Ben and Claire had not seen each other for many days now, as Claire had been away with Kate, and then there was work. But today, Ben had called to say that there was nothing he would enjoy more than an opportunity to see her, to linger over coffee with conversation.

Things had not exactly gone as planned. The lingering coffee turned into a forgotten kettle and a trail of clothing leading to the bedroom. They were now peacefully curled up, listening to the sounds of the world passing them by through the open window. They stayed that way until Ben's phone rang.

"I need to take this, Claire. It's the bank calling." He talked with the phone tucked under his chin while he dressed, and she ran to the guestroom to quickly shower and re-dress.

Ben had been her sanity, the one who calmed her mind

and made everything feel wonderfully ordinary. But he was not vanilla—he had depth, and layers, and a hidden wisdom. Ben had a capable way of handling any and every obstacle he encountered, which he had clearly demonstrated in the way he conducted himself at work and the way he raised his son. Being a bank manager also made him a counselor, a doctor, a mediator, and a mentor. People looked up to him, and it was clear why. He was a problem solver with a wit to match Kate's. When she was with him, she felt sane and collected. He was her safety net and lately, Claire found herself wanting his company more and more.

Ben was waiting for her in the kitchen, and they shared a hurried cup of tea. It was later than they realized, and each of them had places they needed to be. As Claire made her way to the door, Ben followed with his hand gently on her back.

"We have not given ourselves much of an opportunity for real conversation. Are things okay? How much are you still wrapped up in that Will thing?"

This was certainly not a subject that could be covered in a couple of minutes standing by the door.

"Let's talk tonight," was all she said. After kissing him goodbye, she left the house, her whole body still feeling flushed. The man had passion! Clara Perova's musical genius unashamedly began humming "Night and Day" by Ella Fitzgerald.

With a twinge of guilt, she entered the office through the rear door, only to run straight into Bert.

"I hear that Tony Conti has opened a new place," Bert said to her, matter-of-factly, as though they had just been in the middle of a conversation. He didn't appear to be in a particularly good mood. "I saw an article in the paper today. The man is swimming in money, and I would like to know where he gets it all. The restaurant business can't be that lucrative. The paper said that this restaurant is to be managed by his wife, Daniela. Great, we get one more restaurant that's Moroccan, Italian, or Asian. Funny, I thought this was Canada!"

This was one of Bert's oddities. Bert's family had themselves emigrated from Turkey and settled in Vancouver to be with relatives. Bert was just an eight-year-old boy when they arrived on Canadian soil, and he had an extremely hard time adjusting to a new country. He was teased mercilessly, and kids often chased him home from school. The experience left Bert with an impaired view of humanity in general. He had confessed to Claire that it took him a long time to feel accepted; unlike her, he might remain forever bitter. The hardest thing about 'having been there' is coming out of that place unjaded.

Given his own experiences, one would think that Bert would be more sympathetic for people who settled into a new land, but it seemed quite the opposite. He had no patience whatsoever for immigrants. Maybe it was symbolic. His anger and hostility toward them might be related to the injustice that his family had suffered at the hands of those who were meant to welcome them into this country, even if it was likely just a handful of mean school kids. The man carried a lot of anger inside. Claire wondered if his breath smelled of alcohol today as well.

In all the time Claire had worked with him, this was the closest she had come to verbalizing any criticism of Bert. Claire had long felt that Bert's prejudices extended far outside the parameters of racism. He also detested anyone with great wealth, even his own clients. He had grown up poor. As hard as he worked, he would never have what those families had amassed by passing things along through the generations—businesses, estate homes, or what have you. These people could buy cars and houses for their children when they came of age, but Bert felt the children should be forced to work for it.

Everyone went back to work. Ruth looked like she would cry. None were oblivious to his brash and unwelcome sermon.

It was then that Bert walked to the window and said, "So, I see they've left. For a while, I thought they might be coming in."

"Who are you talking about, Bert?"

"There were two men parked out there, they must've sat there for a good twenty minutes. I thought they were coming in to discuss some real estate or something, but they're not there anymore."

"Two men? Isn't it a bit odd, Bert, that two men would be sitting in a car just outside our door?" Claire lifted her head and ventured, "Out of curiosity, did you happen to see what they looked like?"

"Just a couple of guys. Actually, they could have been related, they kind of looked the same. I don't think I've ever seen them around this area before. Oh, and I remember—they had red hair. That's too bad, I thought maybe they were going to give us some business."

Claire felt her blood go cold.

Chapter 28

A CLOUD CROSSED CLAIRE'S FACE. THE NEWS DIDN'T SIT well with her. So, now there had been three sightings of these men. Who were they, and who was on their radar now? Claire knew that it was time to have another conversation with Wolf, as this was something that he should be aware of. But she already had something else on her mind. Sitting down at her desk, she had opened her paper to the local stories and the headline read, 'Driver identified from car crash two days ago.' Scanning the article, she came to the name: Maria Dieno.

The article went on to say that the woman was in hospital in intensive care, having undergone surgery, and her condition was listed as critical. The authorities were pleading for witnesses who may have seen the accident to come forward. The single-vehicle crash was described as being "suspicious." Apparently, there were no skid marks—her car had simply left the road and hit a tree on the other side of the ditch. However, there were marks from a second vehicle that may or may not have been made at the same time.

Claire cleared her schedule for the remainder of the day. Did Maria just drive off the road or was her car pushed? She left a note on Bert's desk and told Ruth she was leaving. With trembling hands she unlocked her car and got into her car. She rushed to the hospital where Maria had been admitted, trying hard to focus on her driving. There were many things racing through Claire's mind as she found a parking spot and hurried into the building. Although she was not able to get inside the ward, she did notice Will's mechanic friend, Glen, sitting in the hallway with a couple that were probably Maria's parents.

Claire quietly walked over to where the three were seated. She said hello to Glen and introduced herself to Maria's parents. Jorge looked so torn up with grief, it was unclear whether he knew which way was up. Teresa, on the other hand, looked at her anxiously, only too eager to talk.

"You know my Maria?"

"She called me two days ago and wanted to talk. I met her for lunch," Claire explained. "Before that, I didn't really know her."

Glen looked at her and said, "Maria had been out to the shop to talk to me and was on her way back to town. She seemed agitated, and she was mumbling something about how she should have stayed home. We are waiting for the doctor to come and talk to us. She was hurt pretty badly, and she is still in intensive care. Doctors had her in surgery yesterday and stopped some internal bleeding. Her organs were pretty damaged, but I'm not sure of the full extent."

Taking her hand, Teresa motioned for Claire to sit beside her, away from Jorge. Glen, sensing this need for privacy, took Jorge down the hall for a coffee and a bite to eat. The man had likely not eaten all day. Teresa told Claire that she had long been concerned about Maria's behavior. She knew certain things that she had not told Jorge. At least six months before

Will's death, she had come home early from work one day and had caught Will and Maria together. Will, like the coward he was, had ran out the side door and was pulling out of the driveway before Teresa had even made it to the front door. Maria had cried and pleaded with her to not say anything to her father, or to anyone.

Teresa explained, "Maria told me that Will had come over to see her one day, about two years ago, when Jorge and I were at work. Maria said that he had come over to check in on her, but I think he knew what he wanted and was out to get it. They started being together soon after that. Maria told me, 'I am older now, Mama, I can do what I want, and I know what I want.' Will had told her that he was no longer married, that he loved her and would take care of her."

Teresa sighed before she went on. "But you must understand, she was still afraid of the men who hurt Elyse. I told her to stop this foolishness, it would kill her father, but she told me that she needed Will. I cringed at this. Why did she use such words? I could see in her eyes that she had disapproved of Will and Elyse because of jealousy, not out of decency. I then ordered her to stop, told her that she was being foolish. But I suspected that she hadn't stopped. How could I monitor her when was an adult and I needed to be at work?"

Claire thought Maria had been holding back when they met, and it was now obvious that she had actually lied to her. The woman had been probing for information when they met. Claire wondered what else she had lied about. This story seemed more in line with what Wolf had told her about Maria and Elyse, especially the fact that they were both interested in Will. Without even searching for them, the truths were coming to Claire.

Teresa looked back to be sure that Jorge and Glen had gone before she continued her story. "The day Maria went to meet you, I came home from work and found her inconsolable, as she had discovered that Will had been seeing you. She said she had asked him about it, and he had denied it. She said that her plan was to meet you to ask if you had knowledge of the men she had seen, but when she realized that you two had been together, she fell apart. You need to understand that Will had money, and she convinced herself that he could protect her, but now she was panicking. The men were still out there somewhere, so when she got in her car today, we asked ourselves why she would risk leaving the house. Glen later told us that she drove out to the shop to ask if he could help her to go somewhere safe."

"Tell me about these men, the ones she thought were after her," questioned Claire, determined to uncover more of Maria's lies. She tried to recall other things that Maria had said to her. "Are these the ones she spoke of, with red hair?"

"I don't think so. I thought this man was big and dark. She said that Elyse's cousin had taken money from a launderer to pay back a loan shark. His plan was to go to Venezuela and bring back drugs, enough to pay everyone. This man Charlie gave Dany a lot of money, but Dany never came back. We understood the ultimatum for Dany was to return their money or come back with the drugs. But nobody had seen Dany. So, they had been watching his apartment ever since he left. This was going on long before Elyse disappeared. These men would have had lots of time to learn who she and Maria were, and why they were there. Maria believed that whoever killed Elyse would kill her too, for they were certain she could recognize them.

"How do you know all this?" Claire asked.

"Maria told me all this. She said that Dany had called her when he heard what happened to Elyse. He was crying and panicked. He then told Maria the story and said that she was still in danger, that she should get out. So for all this time everyone believed that Dany had not come back, but she knew he had. She moved back home soon after that, without a word to us about anything."

Teresa started to cry. "I only found this out a few days ago. Before that, Maria said nothing to me. Jorge and me, I think we didn't want to know. We thought if we just carried on we could go back to normal. Maria started to leave the house months ago, and she would not tell me where she was going. She stopped being careful. She never imagined that he would wait all this time for his opportunity."

Claire felt her brain go into overload. This was a lot of information to digest. It seemed that everyone was hiding something, even from people that they should be trusting. Maria held on to a great deal of knowledge during her silent period, why the sudden desire to blurt it all out? Was it simply because Will had died? She would need to take some time to make sense of it all.

Teresa looked tired and completely defeated. "You see, after Elyse died, her father called his sister in Venezuela and told her the news. He said that they needed to get in touch with Dany right away, as he needed to come and be with his uncle's family and to look after the apartment. Dany was to leave on a flight a few days later, but nobody has seen him. He called Maria only once, but then she heard nothing more from him."

"Did you not go to the police? They could have offered you protection and with Maria's help, they might have stopped whoever was doing this to your family."

"I told Maria that she must go to the police, but she was afraid that the man would come and kill all of us. Dany had said it was better for her to say nothing. Then, she said that the best thing would be for her to go away from here, and that was why she went to see Glen. Now, I need to talk to the police, even though I am afraid. But Jorge will want someone to pay for what they did to our daughter."

The silence surrounding Claire was unbearable. The hallway where they sat was so quiet that she could hear the clock humming on the wall. Feeling shaken and fumbling her words, she got up to leave. She wasn't good at this sort of thing. She was just a photographer. She wished Teresa the best and said that she would check in later to see if Maria was doing any better. She and Jorge had a rough road ahead of them.

As she walked away, Claire kept returning to the same nagging question: if Elyse was killed over Dany's drug money, then why was Will killed? And where was Dany now? The sound of Claire's heels echoed in the stairwell as she made her way into the sunlit parking lot, relieved to be out of the hospital.

Driving away, Claire wondered whether anyone needed to warn Daniela. She was not convinced that there was no connection between the damn redheaded men and this other man. She also had other reasons to be curious about Daniela. Claire disliked herself for thinking it, but… What if she just *happened* to go to the new Osteria?

The rational side of her said "Stay away," but a mixture of curiosity and concern for Daniela's safety was leading her to the restaurant. She made up her mind that she would meander into the restaurant to have a coffee and have a look around. She wasn't even certain that the woman would be there. Yes, Ben and Kate had suggested that she stay away Even so, Claire's respect for their caution would not deter her from this. She that felt this was something she needed to do.

Chapter 29

After dinner that evening, Claire and Kate went to sit outside, where it was cool but pleasant. Claire sheepishly brought Kate up to date with everything that had gone on, still feeling contrite about her involvement with Will. It was difficult being so blunt, but she felt that it needed to be said. She wasn't looking forward to the day when she would share this information with Ben, wondering how he would react to these new revelations.

Kate seemed to sum it up really well: "You know Claire, you shouldn't be so hard on yourself. Affairs are more common than we imagine. It's a part of human nature, and it certainly had nothing to do with you. There was no way you could have known. Also, it has less to do with sex and more to do with Will's insecurity. It's the sexual attraction combined with the thrill of secrecy. The poor guy must have had a screwed-up life to begin with. If he was getting something out of it, maybe he didn't even know what."

After giving it some thought, Claire responded. "He just seemed so confident, so certain of what he wanted and who he was. He presented a very respectable face to the town. Maybe women made him feel so confident. But Kate, he was sleeping with at least three women! One was too young, one was too old and married, and I was the other. I think he was just a total parasite. I guess nothing could protect him from his weakness for women." Oddly enough, Claire felt okay. If she had been attracted to some level of badness about Will, she was certainly cured of it now. It was a good lesson.

"I think Will loved himself enough without needing me to love him as well. I'm not going to try to understand him or how I felt back then. Ben is actually capable of giving love, unlike Will. I need to focus more on Ben now. He loves Adam, and he loves me. I think that he could use some love in return."

"You know I never liked Will, Claire. I didn't trust him either, but you seemed so oblivious to the signs I was picking up. I know it's 1987 and we have sexual freedom and all that, but his needs did seem to be about something else. It's funny, today's catch phrase is 'free sex can kill', what with the risks of diseases and all that. It couldn't have been truer for Will, but unlike anyone could have imagined." Kate looked over at Claire and added, "I'm so glad that Ben is helping you through this. He's patient, and he cares so much about you. I hope you know that."

Claire nodded without speaking. Still, she knew what her next move would be.

It was about a six-kilometer drive to the new restaurant. The town where Claire lived didn't have a lot of space for new business owners, so in the last few years, when a new establishment wanted to open, they were re-directed to a new locale which was becoming well known for its shops and restaurants. The massive sign on the archway at the entrance simply read, "The Square."

She popped in a Bryan Adams cassette and headed out of town. Claire had no idea what to expect, what she would find out, or why she even came in the first place. Perhaps the real reason, if she was being honest, was an opportunity to gain some insight into Will's long-standing relationship with Daniela.

It took Claire some time to find the location, as it was tucked away on the far side of the Square, just off the main road, about a mile from the gas station. Not the most ideal spot, but spaces were at a premium, and they were lucky to have obtained even this location. There was one big advantage, in that they could catch business from people coming off the freeway, as they would be the first visible eatery.

It was unusual to see so much development in this particular area. When Claire was young, her grandfather would often bring her, Tracey, and Paul to this spot to fish from the bridge that extended over the river. This was one of the narrowest sections of the water, and at the time, the banks were grassy, with a gradual slope to the water. Grandfather would put the worms on their hooks, and they would stand patiently at the water's edge, casting their lines out and reeling them back in.

After they had fished, they would sit on the grass and eat peanut butter sandwiches that her grandmother had made for them. The sandwiches were soft from the heat, and their bottles of soda pop were warm, but everything tasted so good. They would laugh and tell stories about school and friends. They rarely caught any fish, but the memories of those summers were dearly engraved in her mind.

The shores of the river were now gone, having been built up with huge concrete retaining walls. A new major highway overpass had been installed, and instead of the sloping grassy banks, there were now large concrete culverts. The water was no longer visible unless a driver was to pull over to the shoulder and peer over the edge. There was not the slightest recognizable thing anywhere in the area.

As she pulled into the almost-empty parking lot, she said to herself, "It is the wise man who knows when to distance himself." Yet here she was, perhaps not so wise. Clara Perova sang, "Everybody Plays The Fool, Sometimes." Claire got out of her car, took a deep breath, and headed towards the building. "I should have brought Kate," she mumbled to herself.

Chapter 30

THE OSTERIA WAS QUITE BEAUTIFUL INSIDE, THE HIGH-lights being the backlit shelves of wine and the stately ceramic urns strategically placed on the tables. Striking antique fixtures adorned the walls, the panels painted in muted earthy colours. The unmistakable sound of Eros Ramazzotti singing "Terra Promessa" came from somewhere. This place was pure elegance, right down to the polished cement floors and small tables with roomy comfortable chairs.

Quickly scanning the room, Claire seated herself at the first table she saw. Appreciating the luxurious glow of the lighting, she thought about how lovely this place would be for an intimate evening dinner. Aside from another couple seated in the heart of the restaurant, she was the only other patron. This made her nervous, but she figured that it was highly unlikely that Daniela knew who she was.

Claire certainly recognized her right away, though. She stood by the bar with her head bent over some papers. Daniela was a fifty-ish raven-haired Italian spitfire. Something about her sexuality immediately recalled a very voluptuous Sophia Loren in one of those Italian movies. She was an older woman who knew who she was. She exerted her prowess over all the young men in some little Italian cafe, holding a silver tray of wine as she winked and flirted over her shoulder.

Daniela wore a pair of skinny jeans and a white silk shirt with just the appropriate number of open buttons. It would not have generally suited someone of her age, but it was somehow striking on her. Daniela came over to Claire's table once the other couple had left, with eyes full of contempt. Or maybe that was just eyeliner, of which there was certainly plenty. Rather than sit, she stood very close and asked Claire why she was there. She was busted. Ben had told her to stay the hell away from this whole mess, yet here she was.

"I know I shouldn't be here," she sputtered uncharacteristically. "But I'm here about Will, and I think what happened to him may not have been an accident. I guess I just wanted to see if you were okay," she lied. "I wanted to ask if you had noticed anything odd about him the last time you spoke to him." She noticed that Daniela's hair was just a bit too black for a woman her age.

"How dare you come here? What makes you think I spoke to Will? How do you even know that I knew Will? I have nothing to say to you, and I don't have to tell you how inappropriate it is for you to be here."

She was furious as she continued, "These are private matters and to have you, a *stranger*, barge in here like this and try to cause trouble is not appreciated."

"I think I should leave" Claire quickly stood up and tried to walk past Daniela. "I am so sorry to have bothered you."

"Yes, you should leave. There's the door, and it would be in your best interest to not come back." Daniela spat out the words, almost literally.

Holding her stance, Claire needed to get the words out. "Daniela, do you know anything about two men with red hair?"

"What do you mean, two men with red hair?" Daniela was suddenly not talking, but listening.

Claire explained, "It's probably nothing, I had just heard something about two men who had been at Will's."

"And from exactly whom did you hear that from?" questioned Daniela.

Claire was not about to reveal what Wolf had told her, and she was immediately sorry she that had mentioned it. "You know what? Forget it. It's just a stupid rumour, and there's likely no truth to it. I've caused you enough grief, and I am going now." This woman seemed capable of looking after herself and didn't appear to be in any need of protection. On the contrary, Claire almost pitied anyone who would try to cross her.

Daniela positioned herself precisely in front of Claire, face to face. Claire noticed that her lips seemed locked in a pouty expression. Probably from years of practice, they had become permanently frozen in that position.

"Look, you stupid girl, don't try to solve my mysteries for me or somehow fix my life. You don't know anything about me, and you don't know anything about Will. Now please, get out."

"Gee, Daniela," Claire said to herself. "Please don't hold back! Tell me how you really feel."

Doing the quickstep, Claire exited the bistro while mumbling "Beat It" by Michael Jackson. She didn't stop moving all the way to her car, cursing herself. "Well, you handled that with the finesse of a ten-year-old," she muttered. She got into her car and drove away without looking back. How could Will have given up his family for such an abhorrent creature?

When she was certain that Claire had left, Daniela went back to the kitchen. Once she had regained some composure, she exited the back door, to the parking lot, where she then entered a separate building. Inside that building was Tony's small office. She immediately went over to his desk, picked up the phone, and dialed a number. "I think we have a problem," she said. "Can you come over tomorrow?"

Chapter 31

WALKING ALONG THE LAKE, CLAIRE'S MIND FLASHED BACK to her childhood. She had all too many recollections of the children whose lives were lost here during the winter months. Some of those kids had been her friends. She remembered how they came in droves with their ice skates whenever the lake froze. Some of them came too early in the season, when the shoreline areas had not yet been hit with the freeze necessary to make the banks sturdy enough. Weak spots in the ice couldn't take the impact of kids piling on top of one another.

Also, during the summer months, there were those that opted for homemade rafts that didn't always prove to be stable or seaworthy. One of her classmates, Bryan, had been one of those kids to die on a raft one summer. He was Kate's cousin. She recollected watching the emergency crews drag the bottom of the lake in search of his small body. He was placed on a stretcher, all white and bloated. It was a horrible memory.

Since Kate now had a new man in her life, Claire had been seeing less and less of her. The solitary feeling in an empty house, with nobody to laugh at your jokes, was something she was not accustomed to. She was missing someone used to be there, and this was different than living alone. She felt that there was a big difference between the two. It was no fun cooking for one and having her meals alone. So, she had asked Ben to meet her at the lake. Claire had suggested the walk, as it was a better to update him in person than over the phone. Plus, she thought the air would help to clear her head.

"Ben, Maria's still not out of danger, even if she lives. Look at her! What she's had was not a life, but more like a prison. I think someone tried to murder her. I'm grateful that the police are involved, glad that Teresa told them everything."

"Now you are talking about murder and danger? What exactly have you been up to?"

She then proceeded to tell Ben the whole story. She told him of her conversations with Maria, Wolf, and Bonnie. This time she didn't leave anything out. Then, she told him about Maria's accident and the connection to Elyse. She concluded with the conversation she and Teresa had at the hospital. He listened to her story incredulously. By the time she was finished, they were seated on a bench overlooking the lake.

When she finally stopped, he sat back in disbelief. "When did you have time to work?" he asked. She smiled at the remark; Ben was so good-natured and endearing. He was so unlike Will. What she had discovered about Will had been an epiphany. He was the antithesis of everything Ben was.

"I get it, Claire. I get that you wanted to help these people. But Jesus, you have to let it go! It's getting dangerous, and I can't take much more of this."

"I honestly don't know how this happened, Ben. People just started coming to me and telling me things. Was it that obvious that I wanted to know more? With Wolf, it was more a case of each being afraid of the other, and it was so good that he came to me. There's something about Wolf that really puts me at ease, Ben. Out of all of this, he was the only glimmer of sanity. Sometimes trusting is hard enough, let alone knowing who to trust. That can be even harder. I would really like to talk to him again."

"But you are not a detective, Claire." Ben was looking at her with genuine concern.

"My interest in this has long ago stopped being about Will. The man is offensive beyond words, so why should he go down as some sort of notable town figure with a legacy? But now, I can't imagine what it's like for the families of Maria and Elyse."

"So why on earth did you go to see this woman, Daniela?"

"I don't know. Maybe I thought she might be in danger as well. Or maybe she knew something about the two weird guys out there somewhere. Going to see her is my one regret. Okay, my second regret, if you know what I mean. I really had no business being in that place. She's a most reprehensible character, and she scared the hell out of me."

"Has it ever dawned on you that you are also in danger from these men? You seem preoccupied with saving everyone but yourself." Ben seemed angry, and it was the first time she had really seen him assert himself in this way.

"Yes, I have thought about that. But I thought that if anyone wanted to hurt me it would have happened by now."

Tensing, Ben turned his whole body to face her. "Seriously?" was all Ben could manage.

They sat there for a while longer, each lost in their thoughts, as they watched the city trucks begin setting up orange traffic cones for the upcoming Gay Pride parade. The theme for the parade was "Coming Together." Claire thought these to be wise words for everyone. These were great strides forward for the gay community and, looking back, they didn't deserve the horrors that had happened to them in Toronto over the years. Theirs was an uphill battle for equality, social acceptance, and the freedom to be. "We are all different, yet we all fight for the same things," Claire said to herself. She should invite Bert to the parade. Her gaze took her back to Ben where he sat in silence. He didn't look happy.

Chapter 32

After finishing up with the yard work, Claire made her way inside, where she showered and changed into sweats and a t-shirt. She came downstairs and poured herself a glass of wine while she pondered her dinner choices. On the days when Kate was away, Claire had less of an appetite, so she settled on a sandwich, however unlike her it was. She turned on some music and busied herself in the kitchen. Might as well make it a *good* sandwich.

There were some photographs in the dark room that needed her attention. Her new shots of Rocky Ridge were drying. They looked splendid, and the developers would be pleased. Kate had generously agreed to turn their laundry room into a dark room for Claire. With a few simple modifications it had worked out perfectly. It had to be this room, as she needed both ventilation and water. With the help of Kate's brother, a suitable laundry room was installed at their back-door entrance, which offered the necessary enclosed space. While the area was much smaller, they had agreed that laundry was a necessity and not a place that needed to be glamorous.

Cleaning up the dark room would also be necessary, as Claire needed to wash out her processing trays, bottles, and funnels. But first, she needed wine and sustenance. She went to the living room and turned on the television so she could listen while she finished up in the kitchen. She then placed her meal and her glass of wine on a tray and headed for the sofa in the next room, to watch the evening news. It was beginning to get dark outside, a sure sign of the rapidly progressing fall season. This was not her preferred method of dining, nor was it her finest meal creation, and she properly admonished herself. She couldn't remember Kate's schedule for the day and was unsure when to expect her, so she had prepared nothing for her friend. The kitchen counter was left riddled with her mess. There were crumbs, an open jar of mustard, and a large mayonnaise-stained knife on the cutting board.

"I'm sure to become a slob if Kate ever leaves," she laughed to herself. Carefully balancing the tray as she walked across the room, she set it on the coffee table. She then settled in to watch her favourite news program.

Just as she picked up her sandwich, she heard a something strange from the other room. She turned down the volume to listen more closely. Sure enough, there was a scraping noise at the other side of the house. It sounded like it was coming from the window in the dining room. That part of the house was easily accessible from the street if someone walked around the small bush beside the garage. Startled, Claire put her plate down and very slowly stood up. This didn't sound good.

The phone was in the kitchen and she would have to pass the doorway to that room to get to it. She crouched down against the floor and hazarded a peek. There was definitely a figure trying to pry the window open. Whoever was out there was concentrating on the clasp. Hoping he was distracted enough not to notice, she crouched down and passed by quickly, unseen.

Trying not to panic, she quickly walked over to grab the phone and dialed 911. With pounding heart she waited for someone to answer. Feeling a good dose of impatience, she went through all of the preliminary questions asked by the dispatch person. She was becoming increasingly agitated at the length of time that this seemed to be taking. What was likely minutes seemed like hours. The intruder could be in the kitchen by the time the dispatcher got on with it.

After what seemed an eternity, she hung up the phone with news that the police were on their way. She had a sinking feeling that they might not arrive in time. She thought to call Ben next, but she was disappointed when her call was taken by his answering machine. "Where are you?" she pleaded. "Someone is trying to break into my house, and I'm in the kitchen." Hanging up, she decided that she needed another plan. She debated exiting through the back door, but there was really nowhere to go. The rear fence was too high, and the only other way out was by the very spot where the intruder was working. Glancing at the knife on the counter she could only think to herself, 'No way *that's* gonna happen.'

Pausing to collect her thoughts, she then decided to run out the front door and get into her car. She could likely get there before the person saw her. Just then, she heard the sound of breaking glass. The intruder had lost patience with trying to pry the lock and had given up on stealth. Grabbing her keys from her purse which was luckily on the hook by the laundry room, she once again crouched past the line of visibility and headed for the front door. She bolted outside without closing the door behind her and ran right into a man who was standing right there. She screamed.

Claire was grabbed firmly by the shoulders by a second person., "Claire, what the hell is going on?" a voice called out to her. It was Kate and her new man, Philippe, whom she had almost knocked off his feet.

"Someone is at the side, they are trying to break in. I called 911, but I don't know when they will be here." She could hear the panic in her own voice.

Philippe ran to the side of the house but came back shortly after, saying he found no one there. Kate took a very rattled Claire back into the house and sat her down. Minutes later, a police car arrived. The police inspected the side of the house and checked the yard before coming inside. Tediously, Kate, Philippe, and Claire needed to give their statements, which fortunately didn't take long. The two police officers then left. Philippe walked them out to their cruiser and stayed for a few minutes talking to them.

Philippe came back into the kitchen, accompanied by Ben. He hurried over to her, a concerned look on his face. "I came here as soon as I got your call. Philippe told me everything, Claire. Are you okay?"

"I don't know what the hell is going on, Ben. I feel a little silly but I was really scared."

Philippe went for one last check of the dining room windows. Kate had pulled all the blinds and re-checked the window locks. Coming back into the kitchen, she introduced Philippe to Claire and Ben. Glad to finally have a proper introduction to this guy, Claire warmly shook his hand. With a feeble smile and an attempt at humour, she said, "How do you like me so far?"

He presented as a staggeringly charismatic man with a big voice and an easy-going manner. Claire felt an incredible ease around him. She detected a slight accent, perhaps French-Canadian. He had somewhat of a Beach Boys look, with curly blonde hair, a white shirt, and darkly tanned skin. Claire almost expected him to have a surfboard tucked under his arm. "That's okay, I thought you ran out because you were just happy to meet me," he teased. Claire smiled.

"You will now be impossible to live with. You'll never believe that this was a random burglary," lamented Kate. "I know it was scary, but we don't know that it wasn't just a local kid taking a chance that nobody was home."

Not wanting to upset her friend, and genuinely wanting to believe that she was right, Claire agreed that she would not jump to conclusions. Ben and Philippe echoed Kate's sentiments. As there was nothing more to say this evening. Ben stood to leave. Philippe rose also, saying it was late and Claire should get some rest. Claire and Kate walked the men to the door, Ben promising to call her as soon as he got home.

The night brought little sleep for Claire. Ben had been so kind when he called to say goodnight. She didn't want to believe that she'd managed to get herself in over her head, despite the warnings from her friends. There was no valid reason for anyone to want to break in and harm her. Yet she wondered if she could have carelessly exposed herself to danger. Surely all of her actions had thus far been harmless?. Was she missing something? She would love to know who tried to break in and whether the two men with red hair were involved.

She rolled over in bed, pulled the covers over her head, and cried. She cried because she was afraid that she almost lost her life. She cried for her grandparents who had lost theirs, and she sobbed for Oliver, whom she had left behind. Where was her Oliver? Was he somewhere on a beach, sipping ouzo at sunset, someone new by his side? Was he missing her? Had she been wrong to leave him behind? Perhaps he was right when he said that she could do nothing for her grandparents. She seemed to have been sabotaging her own happiness.

"Be careful and don't be a foolish girl," her grandmother instilled in her. *Ne bud glupoy devochka.*

Claire never could have imagined that those would be the last words she ever heard from her.

Chapter 33

Wolf was driving into the gas station just on the edge of town. He often took this route as there was always less traffic and he could get home much more quickly. Continuing on this road would also take him past the Osteria Bistro, which up until now had meant nothing to him, and he never gave it a second glance. However, today when he drove by, he noticed two men in the parking lot. He looked closer and was struck with how much they looked like the same two men he saw the night Will died.

They were deeply involved in dialogue with someone inside a parked vehicle, who was obstructed from his view. On impulse, Wolf kept his head down, although he was not certain why. Wolf could feel his blood begin to boil. This town was too small for all of this shit to be going on, and this certainly wasn't representative of life here. How could one go about just living in peace anymore?

Reflecting on his conversation with Claire, he wondered if he should have told her about Will's infidelity with the arrogant woman who owned this place. There seemed no need to bring it up at the time, and likely there was no need now. Will may have died, but it looked as if his problems might not have died with him. Wolf had long wanted to slap some sense into Will, but it wouldn't have changed anything. A new thought immediately crossed his mind. If the men had unfinished business with Will, did that mean that now they were snooping around anyone who had contact with him?

This was turning into a little horror show. How could activities of this nature be going on in this peaceful town? How could people like this end up here, disrupting the order of things? Wolf had no idea whether he himself was in any imminent danger, but he also had Ilse to worry about. Wolf didn't slow down; he kept driving. Maybe he had been taking this too lightly from the beginning. He needed time to think, and he wanted to get home.

Since marrying and moving to the area, Wolf and Ilse immensely enjoyed their lives within this community. They tended not to have many friends in their home neighborhood, but they did have hospitable and good-natured neighbours. Wolf would often be seen in the roadway, chatting with the other men while out cutting the grass or taking in the trash cans after collection. On hot evenings, someone would always host a bonfire and beer event, to which Ilse loved to bring some of her famous pretzels.

Wolf and Ilse were quite connected to the German Club in the suburbs of Toronto, and over the years had attended many of the events held there. This included everything from dinner and dance evenings, to summer picnics in designated parks, to the occasional outing to the symphony. Nearby Durham County held equestrian events, in which Ilse was deeply involved. There were many venues within a reasonable distance, which allowed her ample opportunities to ride.

Life is strange, the way it draws us to certain people and causes a protectiveness we didn't know we had. He did not have a sister growing up, nor did he have a daughter. Yet, Wolf felt an undeniable kinship to the lovely golden-haired Claire. Their conversations flowed, they saw eye to eye on many things, and they had even finished each other's sentences on occasion.

Theirs was an unusual bond considering they had grown up so differently and were years apart in age. Wolf decided that he would make a point of calling in to see Claire tomorrow. Wolf felt that he needed to act quickly and scolded himself for not calling the police long ago. He decided to speak with Claire and suggest that they do so now.

Chapter 34

CLAIRE SAT IN HER CAR, UNABLE TO MOVE. SHE HAD ALWAYS been the one who stood back and recognized solutions to problems that others couldn't see. She was always the sensible one who had the answers. She went over the past few months in her mind, and she searched for any explanation for her inability to distance herself from Will's death. What was keeping her from letting it go? There was still a nagging suspicion that the dots could connect, if only she could figure out how. Maybe it was just one missing dot.

For whatever reason, she had been peeking into some portal, hearing secrets that were not hers to hear. She was torn between compassion and the instinct to flee. She had grown up in her little bubble, sheltered from the evils of the world. This is the kind of thing that her parents had always tried to protect her from. I suppose they did love her very much, but she had just been a typical antagonistic teenager. Looking through a new lens, Claire was learning that the real world is a scary place.

She had been raised with certain values and morals, and she had no idea how to gauge them against others. She had to be careful in her judgments: for all of the Wills, Berts and

Daniellas out there, there were also the Bens, Kates, and Wolfs. When she weighed the balance, she realized that her life was peaceful and uncomplicated. Now, Tracey's life with Bob and their kids didn't look so bad. There was something to be said for safety and stability. Claire herself had no problems to speak of, until that dance last summer. She had fallen under Will's and, as a result, had found herself in the sad and messy lives of others. Clara Perova, Musical Director Extraordinaire (though she feeling less than extraordinaire today), was playing 'Reflections of My Life,' by Marmalade.

Claire loved her life and those in it, and she craved a return to normalcy. It made her crazy to think that she came close to giving up Ben for a shallow fantasy. She felt that she had come close to losing her life the night of the attempted break-in. She was certain that someone had come to harm her. It was time for her to let go of the search. *I need to call the police*, she thought to herself as she picked a piece of lint from her sweater. She started the engine and slowly drove away. Despite not having an appetite, Kate and Philip would be waiting for her for their lunch date.

Later that same afternoon Claire received a call. It was almost immediately after arriving back at the real estate office. A woman's voice said, "I don't have a lot to say to you, but if you are still looking for a tip about the two men you asked about, I may have some important information for you." Claire wasn't certain that it was Daniela, although the voice certainly sounded like hers. Her manner was very hurried, almost frightened. Still, this was good news.

Contrary to all the things she had said to herself this morning, she was back in the here and now, and she wanted answers. This could be all she needed to finally get some closure. When this was all over, she was going to find Ben, throw her arms around him, and end her obsession once and for all. She wanted a life with Ben and Adam. Maybe she even wanted some tin cans clanking against the back of the car as the three of them drove away into the sunset. She wanted to be the kind of woman who baked cookies for the kids playing ball in the park behind her house.

Daniela had asked to meet her at the end of the street. "In ten minutes," she had said. "By the bus stop." She said that she wouldn't wait, and that this was her only chance—if Claire didn't show up, Daniela would say the conversation never happened. So, Claire put on her coat and, with a brief explanation to Ruth, hurried out the door. Her heart was pounding so hard that she was almost gasping for air.

Claire arrived at the corner but saw no sign of Daniela. The bus stop was on the other side of the street. She was halfway across the intersection when she saw a man with red hair standing beside a phone booth. He was right there on the other side of the street, staring right at her. She panicked and froze on the spot. That's when she heard someone call her name. She tried to take a step backwards, but as she turned her head to look, the truck hit her from the other direction. As her body was hurtled through the air, she heard a sound—someone screaming—and then everything went dark.

Chapter 35

CLAIRE OPENED HER EYES. EVERYTHING AROUND HER WAS white, and she thought she was dead. She tried to open her eyes. Everything was blurry, but she could tell that she was definitely in a bed. She heard Kate's voice, then her eyes closed again.

Three days later, Claire woke up. Ben was holding her hand.

"I thought I was dead," she whispered.

"You are very much alive," whispered Ben. "You've been here for some time now, on some pretty heavy meds, so you have slept a lot, no doubt."

"I don't remember what happened to me, Ben. Why am I here?"

"You were run over by a jeep and not by accident. It was those two buffoons, the ones you have been talking about. These two apparently can't do anything right." He offered her a sip of water. "On the bright side, it didn't take them very long to roll over on Daniela. They said that she wanted you dead. She is incensed and has denied everything, of course. I hope she wasn't paying them a lot of money, they're not very competent."

"Daniela? I don't know what you mean."

"We've been lucky that Philippe has been able to provide us with details that have yet to be revealed to the public. For example, Daniela really wanted them to kill you. Did you hear what I said, Claire? *Kill* you." Ben's voice went up a few octaves. "Not just because of your relationship with Will, but because you had come snooping around, asking questions about the goons. She certainly didn't want that to get out."

He quieted down as he remembered where he was. "Daniela must have been a lonely, bitter woman," he said in almost a whisper.

"Ben, I know what you must think of me right now, and I am so sorry."

"It's over now, hopefully. Their story was that Daniela had already lost her husband to his nightclubs, and she didn't want to lose Will too. She had him followed and discouraged anyone who he got close to. It's eerily like that Blondie song, "One Way Or Another." It's very disturbing, Claire. You see, Tony recruited girls like Elyse, and he was known for sampling the goods, so to speak. Daniela endured and Tony denied. Such was their life, but she put up with it because of her life-style, generously paid for by Tony's wealth. He was bringing in a bundle and she had disposable amounts to play with and lavish herself with the best of everything."

"How did you find all this out?" asked a dumbfounded Claire.

"Philippe knows amazing people!" replied a wide-eyed Ben. "I can't ever thank him enough. So anyway, one day, Daniela's mechanic announced that he was going out of business. Shortly afterwards, Will became her new mechanic, and it was like she won a door prize. She was immediately attracted to him, and he with her. She felt justified having this relationship as some sort of retaliation against Tony. This was her payback. And, of course, Will in his endless arrogance was easily led." Ben was enjoying this part.

"So, for years everything hummed along to her satisfaction, but she became incensed when she became suspicious about Will and Elyse. She intended for the boys to warn her away, but someone else got to her first, and they killed her before Daniela's goons could talk to her. At least, this is their story. They said that they were confused about who did it and why, but Daniela didn't care. All that mattered was that the girl is gone. Do you believe it Claire? Such disregard for human life!"

Ben paused while a nurse came in to take Claire's temperature and give her some fresh water. Once she had left the room, he continued.

"For years after that, things were okay for Daniela. She and Will carried on as usual. That is, until you came along. It didn't take her long to find out, especially after you had visited him at the cottage. We won't talk about that bit, okay Claire? Anyway, that was her domain, you see."

"I think Will was a sick man," said Claire, visibly regretful of her involvement.

"Something about Will defying her in this way suggested that he might break away from her, that he was becoming bored with their arrangement. She was afraid of losing him, but she was also angry. So, these same boys were meant to go over and have a little chat with him, to teach him a lesson. It seems that they didn't handle that very well. Those two are a couple of real winners, if you ask me. I don't think they had intended to kill Will, but rather than try to help him, they ran. And in doing that, they basically killed him."

Ben paused for her reaction. Claire wasn't sure how to react, as Wolf had already explained this part to her, and she was sorry she had withheld this from Ben. Looking up at him she nodded in confirmation.

Seeing that she was okay, he continued, "Daniela never would have found out who you were, except that she saw you leave Will's one night shortly before he died. Were you there, that night, Claire?" he looked at her imploringly.

Claire looked down at her hands and Ben had his answer.

"Anyway, she might have let it stop then and there if you hadn't shown up at the restaurant asking questions about her two little friends."

At that moment, Kate walked into the room and went over to give her friend a kiss and a hug. "I'm so glad to see you awake."

She smiled at Ben and sat down to listen to his story.

"But what you don't know is this: if it wasn't for Wolf, you might not be here right now. He saw the two guys the day before your accident, parked at the Osteria. He recognized them from Will's and was pretty sure they were in conference with Daniela."

Kate added, "we ran into Wolf on his way back from our house after we had lunch. He came to see you, but I told him that you were back at your office. He left our house and while heading into town, he saw the men again, only this time they were in a car with Daniela. So, he turned around and drove straight over to your office. When Ruth told him that you had just left on foot to respond to an unusual phone call, he ran out the door after you, urging Ruth to call the police right away."

Looking over at Kate, Ben picked up the dialogue. "Wolf

shouted to you as you walked out into the intersection and after you were hit, he grabbed one guy and held him until the police came. There were witnesses to describe the driver and plenty of helping hands to call an ambulance for you."

"I'd really like to see him, Ben."

"He's coming tomorrow, and he's bringing his wife, Ilse. He said you would understand why."

Claire smiled. "Wolf said that she and I are alike in many ways. He mentioned that he would like us to meet."

"He's a nice man, Claire. He's been here every day. You were right about him, and I think you have yourself a wonderful new friend. So, it looks like there is a bright side to this whole affair, after all."

Chapter 36

Kate let out an audible sigh that reverberated through her body, causing Claire and Ben to look over at her. "So, all of this was because of one wretched and bitter woman. She became a stalker. Like the song said, 'If the lights are all out, I'll follow your bus downtown.' This has been a spine-chilling experience. All of this has happened because of jealousy?"

"But I still don't get it. What about Elyse and Maria?" asked Claire.

"Apparently, the incidents are unrelated," emphasized Kate. "Philippe said that while Will's screwing around may have connected them, the rest appears to be linked to Dany and stolen money. Elyse's death was a tragedy, and Maria got dragged down with everyone else. It is curious, however, that the men didn't kill Will as well. After all, he was around both girls and could have been privy to whatever was going on."

"I'm sure the police will work that one out. Maria's problems might not be over. But hopefully yours are," said Ben with a sigh of relief.

Kate looked at Claire. "You don't look too bad. White becomes you," she commented, tongue firmly planted in cheek. "You had a pretty major concussion, a few broken ribs, a sprained wrist, and a broken ankle. You were very lucky, Claire. The doctor says that you will need to take it easy for a few months to let your body heal. It seems you were luckier than Maria, at least—she is still in a coma."

After Kate said her goodbyes and promised to return soon after work, Ben came and sat by her side again. She appreciated that he didn't push the issue of the time she had spent with Will. She and Ben had no real commitment to each other back then, although the change in their relationship had become apparent over the past months. She loved his new protective side and the way he included her in Adam's life.

Ben interrupted her thoughts. "If the offer still stands, how about that visit to England? Maybe once you are well enough, we should plan the trip. I would love to meet your brother, Paul. Besides, I think that we could both use a vacation, and it will be a good opportunity for Adam to meet your nephew."

Claire closed her eyes and her face broke into the biggest smile she'd had in a very long time. She felt a powerful sense of relief—she was *alive*. No matter the circumstances, it was a very good day. "Yes," she nodded. She was now very tired and promptly fell back asleep. She slept soundly until morning.

Claire was now in her wheelchair, and she had been sitting by the window with Wolf for almost an hour. He and Ilse had come in early in the morning, just as she was waking up, and she wanted to be up sitting with them. Ilse had left after a short time, while Wolf remained to have a longer visit.

"So, have you ever thought about contacting Oliver?" Wolf was asking.

"This sounds juvenile, but he could have called me too. It would have been easier for him to find me, as I lived at home for a long time after returning. It would be harder for me to try to track him down, or so I have always told myself. He could have used the guise that he wanted to return all of my photos and rolls of film. I do wish I had those. I never thought to bring them with me. Anyway, now it's too late, I've moved on with my life. I'm sure he has as well."

Just then, a well-dressed man walked in, accompanied by an equally well-dressed black woman. "Excuse the interruption, but are you Clara Perova?" asked the woman. Claire noted that she was very attractive. She had deep-set hazel eyes and lovely cheekbones. Her skin was radiant, and her generous lips had a natural rosy glow. Hers was a very kind face.

"Yes, I am. Can I help you?" Claire sat up straighter and turned to face the two.

"I am Detective Preston, and this is my colleague, Detective Traviss," as she motioned to her partner. "Might we have a word with you about your accident?"

Wolf stood up to leave, but Claire implored him to stay, saying that it would make it easier for her to have someone with her.

The detectives dragged some chairs from the far end of the room and settled beside her.

"Please start at the beginning and tell us everything you can remember about what happened," prompted Preston. She presented as a highly professional woman, yet retained an air of friendliness. Claire wanted to imagine that under different circumstances, they could have been friends.

This was becoming a normal occurrence for her. Claire had spent her lifetime in peaceful anonymity, and now this was the third time she has been involved with the police. But she immediately felt at ease with these two, unlike the police officer that had questioned her at home following Will's death. She started her story with the eve of Will's death and continued through to her conversation with Teresa Dieno, stopping to introduce Wolf at the appropriate time. It provided the perfect opportunity for the two of them to be questioned at once.

"Why on earth did you not report this sooner?" asked Detective Traviss, exasperation in his voice.

"Because I didn't know if there was anything going on. Not really. All I had were speculations and theories."

The detective then looked at Wolf and asked him why he also had not reported this to the police.

"I was afraid for my wife and for myself. And because they physically did nothing to Will, I had no idea what was their real intent. I too only had theories."

Detective Preston sighed in frustration as she took over the conversation.

"But folks, this is what we do. We investigate theories. People don't always understand that, and they often see us as the bad guys. Even the tiniest, seemingly unimportant thing can mean a great deal to an investigation. We are trained at this and believe it or not, sometimes we do it well. People need to trust us on this," she half smiled as she offered some levity to the situation. "But these men are not why we are here. They are out of our jurisdiction, and they will be dealt with by the local authorities. If they watched a man drown, I would say they are not entirely innocent."

"But who are they?" asked Claire. "Why are they popping up everywhere scaring everyone?"

"We can't answer that question, I'm afraid. They have not been publicly identified yet. But like I said, you people have not been making this easy for us. The York County Police have spoken with Bonnie and have also taken her statement. Today we will speak with Teresa, although her day is off to a tragic start—unfortunately, her daughter Maria succumbed to her injuries this morning. So, our main focus will be to find the man that ran her off the road."

Claire gasped with shock. Poor Maria was dead. Her parents would be inconsolable. She remembered Jorge's face in the hospital, the fear for his daughter evident in his eyes.

"Please, folks, if you think of anything else at all, you must call us right away," added Detective Traviss.

"But what about Daniela?" asked Claire.

"Again, we need to leave Daniela Conti for the local authorities to deal with. We are only here because we needed to investigate the possibility of a connection between your hit and the hit on Maria. But we are with Toronto Detective Operations, so this is out of our jurisdiction. At this point, we can't link the two incidents, so you likely won't hear from us again."

Detective Preston was the first to stand. "We'd better let you get some rest now. We need to go back and focus on Maria and establish some sort of timeline since she left Toronto. You take care of yourself, and you too, sir," she added with a nod to Wolf.

"If there is any way you can give me an update at some point, it would be hugely appreciated. This is connected to me in some way, and I need to know if I might still be in danger," Claire looked at Detective Preston beseechingly. She felt that it would benefit her if she could develop some instant rapport with this woman.

"I can't make any promises, but I know how to reach you," was all she offered, but Claire was sure she caught a hint of agreement in the woman's eyes.

Then, with Detective Traviss looking at both Claire and Wolf reprovingly, the two excused themselves and left.

Claire and Wolf were left with their thoughts.

"I suppose we weren't even honest with each other, let alone with the police," she stated sheepishly. "I trusted the wrong person."

"I don't think it was wrong to have been cautious. Although, it was Hemingway who said 'The only way to know if you can trust someone is to trust them.' And you felt you needed to trust something. It just doesn't always work out. Our thoughts were of surviving and protecting those we love. Not unlike what this Teresa was doing, I would gather," mused Wolf.

With that, Wolf stood to leave. Claire smiled at her friend. She loved his philosophizing nature, his wise and rational mind.

Clara Perova, in a dramatic conclusion, softly sang her song for the moment: "Nobody Told Me There'd be Days Like These," by John Lennon. Wolf turned to her, smiled, and said, "Strange days indeed."

Giving Claire a hug, he said goodbye, promising to call soon.

Chapter 37

THE DAY BEFORE CLAIRE WAS RELEASED FROM THE HOSPI-
tal, Philippe visited with good news. By some stroke of luck,
someone had witnessed the hit on Maria and was able to give
a vehicle description and partial plate number. He went on to
say that it took a while, but the plate number was traced and
registered to a dry-cleaning service in Toronto, owned by
a man named Charlie Winter. Charlie was already a person
of interest and had been for some time. Apparently, he was
a suspect in connection with the murder of a young boy,
Mateo Berger.

"Charlie had been best buddies with one of the men
who was charged with Mateo's murder, but this man and his
accomplice managed to skip town and head out west. The
sexual abuse and murder of this boy was a huge thing, Claire.
There was such outrage to clean up Toronto's streets. It was
the subsequent protests and the politics that actually led to
the raids of some adult shops, shoeshine stands, and body rub
parlours. Did you know that? Eyewitnesses placed Charlie
at the scene, but he was able to provide an alibi, so they had
nothing to charge him with. Since then, it's been a thorn in
the side of the investigating detective, who was dead certain

of Charlie's guilt. When the Soap Raids happened, the detective was still hoping that he could find charges against Charlie. He's been sitting back for years, hoping to get this guy one day," Philippe explained.

"Now that they had an identified vehicle, they dug a little deeper. It led them to the driver on the day of the hit, a man named Otto Pringle, who works for Charlie. The RCMP detectives are investigating him further."

Before Philippe left, he added, "I guess I am fortunate to know people in the system who are more than happy to share updates with me. I never expected to need their help, but it's working out well, don't you think? While my work is not exactly Interpol, we do know a lot, and right now the guys are all over this. I'll let you know if I can find out anything else." A weary Claire uttered her gratitude and felt herself slipping into sleep as Philippe was walking out the door.

Claire spent five days in the hospital before being discharged. Ben and Adam picked her up to take her home. Kate and Philippe were waiting for them. Entering the house took her back to the memory of Will, but she shook it off. She had the feeling that she had been away for a very long time and, oddly, it almost felt like her return from Greece. Having settled on the easy chair, she regarded the activity around her. Watching Kate and Philippe together made her feel like a visitor in her own home. They had fallen into a dance where both shared the leading. She liked it, and it was good to see Kate so happy.

Ben kindly put together a meal for them, and they talked about what would happen next. Philippe had promised to do more poking around at the police department.

"I think that we should buy that friend of yours a bottle of wine or something," offered Claire. "He has been incredibly helpful."

"Or you could offer him your firstborn," Kate helpfully offered.

"Thanks Claire, that would be a nice gesture," responded Philippe with a smile in Kate's direction. "About the wine, that is."

When the meal was finished and all were reposed with their wine, they speculated about the man who drove into Claire. Philippe suggested that he would be charged with vehicular assault causing bodily harm. As for Will, there was no proof that the two of them were even at his cottage that night, except for Wolf's eyewitness account. But even if Wolf could put them there, they didn't come within fifty feet of Will, so they did nothing illegal. They could easily say that they came to have a beer with him. Now, the man who killed Maria was on everyone's mind.

As Claire could do little more than rest, she was inclined to spend more time in front of the television watching the news. The long-awaited headline stated that police had arrested Otto Pringle. As he had no alibi, he was charged with vehicular homicide in connection with Maria. Although they couldn't tie him to the murder of Elyse, they did obtain a search warrant for Charlie Winter's dry-cleaning building, citing a likely connection between the two men and Maria's death. This was a long time coming, and the detectives were celebrating a chance to finally investigate Charlie.

After a search of the building, the police did find large sums of money along, with a small quantity of illegal drugs. The cleaning business was apparently a cover for money launder-ing, drug dealing, and who knows what else. The news story was brief, as Claire knew the police rarely revealed too many details to the public before the case was solved.

Very early the following morning, the ringing of the phone startled Claire. She was pleased when she recognized the voice of Detective Preston on the line.

"I don't have long, but I will give you a brief update so that you won't worry about your safety. We are sure we have our connection, and it does lead us back to Dany and Charlie. We have established that Dany had come to him to borrow money to pay off his gambling debts. Being his boss, Charlie would find a way to make him work it off. Then, Dany disappeared. When he didn't return, the loan shark wanted his money back, as did Charlie. Dany was borrowing from one to pay the other, but paid neither."

The detective paused briefly to see if Claire had a response. When none came, she continued. "We spoke with his father, who said that Dany was trying to come up with the money to pay off his debts after he lost everything at the racetrack. His father was taken by surprise when, without warning Dany, had stolen money from him and had returned to Toronto. Although airport customs clearly indicated that Dany got off the plane in Toronto, he was never seen or heard from. The timeline indicates that he returned after Elyse's body was found. Now that Dany is still missing, it remains unknown whether he is alive or dead. So, you can sleep at night, Claire. We have what we need to work the case."

Kate and Philippe arrived home late the following evening and informed Claire that Otto would be held in custody until his trial. They also told her that Charlie had been arrested during a follow-up search of the dry-cleaning building. While on a perimeter check, one of the detectives noticed a disturbed area at the back of the lot. The ground seemed to be sinking in the corner of the yard and when they called in a team to dig it up, they discovered the gruesome remains of Dany. They were able to identify him by the I.D. in his wallet, which was still in his back pocket. His driver's license, passport, and even his plane ticket were all intact.

"The Coroner's office established that Dany died of blunt force trauma. The unfortunate man's head was almost totally bashed in. They estimated that his death would have occurred approximately four days after he landed at Toronto International Airport," Philippe continued.

"Dany must have returned to his apartment when he arrived back in town. It would have been a foolish move on his part knowing the place might be staked out. We assume someone saw him there and went after him, maybe our friend Otto. When the RCMP searched the place during their investigations, they found a paper with Maria's phone number on it. Otto could have assumed that Dany spoke with her, therefore making it necessary to get rid of her as well."

Claire and Kate looked at him with open eyes.

"Why would she need to die for that?" questioned Kate.

Philippe rubbed his head and looked tired.

"The theory is that Charlie would worry that Dany had revealed too much information to Maria, information that would expose himself and Otto. He couldn't risk her going to the police with their names and the nature of their business. So, now that they had her number, they managed to track down where she lived and followed her, finding the right opportunity to run her off the road."

Claire thanked Philippe again for his ongoing updates. "It is very gracious of you to do this for me, you hardly know me," she said with a smile. She appreciated not having to find these things out through the media.

"I think it's just the right thing to do," he responded.

She went upstairs to lie down and to give Philippe and Kate some privacy.

That evening, Claire sat in the kitchen with Ben while Adam was in the next room colouring with Kate. She rose to check that Adam was out of earshot before continuing any conversation.

"Based on what Philippe said, I still don't know why they killed Dany. A dead Dany can't get them their money back," questioned Claire.

"It's hard to say," answered Ben. "If it wasn't Charlie, it would have been the loan shark that killed him. If Dany didn't die, things may have escalated to the point where the two dealers would have battled it out, each accusing the other of shielding Dany. For all we know, they jointly planned the killing. Killing him showed good faith because Dany had become more a liability than an asset."

"Honour among crooks? Is that what you are saying, Ben?"

"Unfortunately, both camps wanted their money. And Dany stole from them, which is also bad. It's likely a crime punishable by death in those circles. Elyse paid the ultimate price for his indiscretions. And if killing Elyse didn't motivate the kid to get their money, then nothing would. So, maybe they agreed to eliminate the problem by eliminating Dany, even if neither of them could get repaid. This way, neither side could accuse the other of trying to get away with any loot."

"Just think, I would never have been involved in any of this were it not for meeting Will. He wouldn't have either, if he had not offered to help Jorge move some furniture. This is all very tragic, and we can only hope that it will end here."

Claire didn't want to think of the pain that the Dienos would be going through. For reasons unknown, some people are cursed their whole lives, regardless of what they do. Their wounds might never heal but like everyone else, they needed to move forward. We can't erase our wounds—we can only learn to live with them. Her own family had the hardships of war, but the Dienos had their own war. *U vsekh nas bolit,* she could hear her grandfather say to her. We all have pain.

Unfortunately, the drama didn't end there. The following morning headline read that Tony Conti, upon hearing about Daniela and Will, was angered and mortified at his wife's behaviour. Their relationship had taken a major turn for the worse, and the once promising Osteria had closed. Subsequent headlines in the paper announced that Tony was charged with domestic violence after Daniela checked herself into the ER with severe facial lacerations. She arrived at the hospital alone.

"I'll bet the media is loving all of this," said Kate over their morning coffee.

Although one redheaded man was charged with vehicular assault, no charges were brought against his brother. Unbelievably, the two brothers were named Jack and Zack.

"They obviously had parents with a sense of humour," Kate chuckled.

Jack, the one who was charged, didn't turn up for his court

appearance, and the authorities issued a countrywide warrant for his arrest. Claire found it odd that people would be able to leave town so quickly. Did they not own things? She noted that unless they changed their hair colour, they would be easy to spot.

Based on Maria's and Elyse's parents, Charlie and Otto were also investigated for Elyse's murder. Unfortunately, too much time had passed, and there was no evidence to directly link either one of them to the incident. There were no charges laid.

"So much for paying for your crimes," complained Claire.

She cared more about justice for Elyse's sake than she did for Dany's. He was the idiot who was ultimately responsible for the lives of two women.

Claire refused to be an invalid, and she was out of bed as soon as her body would allow. Her wrist and ankle bothered her more than her ribs and head did. The breathing exercises became easier every day, and her ribs were feeling better, but her wrist seemed to be taking forever. She slowly recovered to the point where she could resume a modicum of photography, but she was starting out slowly. She needed to be mobile and use her camera. Although still displaying a slight limp, her ankle felt better before the wrist.

"Too bad my limp is gone," teased Wolf. "We could have gone walking together."

Claire laughed heartily at this, appreciating his humour.

Chapter 38

CLAIRE'S MOTHER, HAVING HEARD ABOUT HER ACCIDENT, had arranged to fly home to be with her daughter. Claire felt very grateful; she had never imagined that she could love and appreciate her mother more than she did right now. Once her mother was satisfied that the damage to her daughter was minimal, she shifted her stance to one of sublime relaxation. They talked like they never had before, and her mother spoke of their life in British Columbia with a new animation. She had also begun to develop a relationship with Ben and Adam, and Claire wasn't sure how she felt about that. She didn't think that her mother developed relationships.

As soon as she was able, she began enjoying long walks with her mother. It became a daily ritual, and it was something that they had not done in the past. Her mother had a new ease about her, which Claire had never seen before. Although she was happy to have her there, Claire felt a little guilty about the timing, being so wrapped up in the ongoing investigations. Her mother was in a perpetual state of disbelief over the things that were going on in her daughter's life.

Kate had not known Claire's mom in her youth, but she was genuinely happy to spend time with her now. She shared stories of school and her antics with Paul during evening meals, which her mother prepared while Kate worked and Claire hobbled around trying to be helpful. Claire often just sat, watching the two women engage in their laughter, and it made her feel good inside.

After weeks of staying around the house, Claire convinced her mother to drive out to visit Wolf and Ilse, wanting very much for her to meet them, and to diversify their days. Ilse and Wolf greeted them outside, and it was soon apparent the two women hit it off. While Ilse was showing her mother the house, Claire and Wolf walked out to see the horses in the paddock. Her heart jumped at the sight of the three animals, who were standing quietly under a tree by the stalls. She walked over to the Andalusian.

"What's her name?" she asked Wolf.

"Karaleen," he replied.

On hearing her name, Karaleen nodded her head with affirmation. Claire was in awe of this spirited horse. She was very tall, taller than any horse Claire had ridden. She rubbed her head into Claire's chest approvingly, causing Claire to laugh, almost giggle with pleasure.

"I am very happy that you are here to see her, Claire. You gave us all a scare, and I am so sorry for what happened to you."

Lost for words, she turned to Wolf, fighting against her tearing eyes and saying nothing. She simply smiled. He leaned over and kissed her forehead. She closed her eyes and accepted the gesture with appreciation.

"And this is Leena, and this one is Ringo," he said as he led her to the other stalls. Claire took her time, stroking each of the animals.

"Come with me," he said after some time.

Wolf then took her to the spot at the end of the paddock, by the fence, where he had watched Will die. She had never seen the view from this side. This was a rare opportunity to imagine that night, with all the performers in place as the drama unfolded. Wolf walked her through the events of that night and when he had finished, Claire shuddered.

"It now seems like an eternity ago, doesn't it, Wolf?"

"To me it seems like yesterday. There has been so much loss of life, and for what? Claire, please don't lose who you are—your essence, your principles. You are a courageous, spirited being, like our Karaleen. Hang onto that."

They turned to make their way back, Claire feeling her eyes start to well up. She felt a sudden chill, and was only too happy to be returning to the house and the welcoming sound of the women's laughter.

After three weeks, her mother packed for the return trip to B.C. The visit had been healing for both women. They had shared meaningful conversations during their time together. On their walks, they had spoken of Oliver, her grandparents, and how important Ben now was in her life.

"Clara, you need to understand that you were very young when you went to Greece, and it was hard on your grandmother. It's not that we didn't like Oliver, but that we hardly knew him."

"When I came back, it was suddenly 'poor Oliver.'"

"But you had made that bed, my dear. When you commit to a life choice, you must really *commit*."

"You were always so hard on me."

"You needed to grow up strong. As women, it's important that we are. It was the best gift I could give you."

"Everything was so confusing back then. I see it now, and although it was a messed up time for me, it wasn't nearly as bad as what these people have gone through."

"You are wiser now. You know what's more important. You know, when we decided to move to the West Coast, I didn't want to go. It was mostly your father, something he had always dreamed of doing. If you had a family—if there had been a baby—I would not have left. But you seemed not to need anyone, least of all me. Even if I truly didn't want to go to Vancouver, I would have followed your father there. *He* is where I belong."

For all of her mother's shortcomings, the woman definitely loved her dad. Claire realized that this was a big part of what love is: their respect for one another, their bond. She must not have had that connection with Oliver—not enough to make her stay with him no matter what. Marriage definitely worked well for some people—particularly those who neither slept around nor lied.

"I want to tell you that you have always been hard on yourself. Perhaps too hard. But you were driven to do well. The life you have built here, with these people, is the best gift you could have given yourself. You have done well, Clara."

Claire saw her mother differently that day. Claire had barely made it through the trauma of dealing with the infidelities of a dead man who she hardly knew. Her mother had lost everything in a war and was uprooted from her country, but she was able to start over again. She may not have been the perfect mother, but she had done the best she could. And what baggage she carried!

The flight was late in the afternoon, and Ben offered to drive. Hugging her mother warmly as they said goodbye at the gate, she promised to come and visit very soon. Adam's tiny hand was clutched tightly to Claire's as he waved to her mom. With teary eyes moistening his cherub cheeks, he whispered goodbye, hardly audibly. Seeing his tears caused Claire's eyes to well up. Ben stood behind the two of them, one hand gently on each of their shoulders.

Christmas was approaching and the memories of the past summer hung over everyone's heads. Without a word, they felt it every time they looked at each other. Although still on leave, Claire did pop into the office on occasion to say hello to Bert, Ruth, and the gang. She had a long-overdue lunch with Tracey at a local restaurant. With Christmas carols blaring over their heads and people crowding every table, it was nice to catch up with her old friend. They agreed to see each other again in the New Year.

Kate and Philippe were the consummate power couple, and Claire was thrilled to see them like this. She reminisced back to the day when Kate had first told her about this new man and the way she had gushed about "How perfect this would be." In true "Kate" fashion, her vision had materialized in exactly that way.

Claire's drug-induced sleeps were a far cry from the many sleepless nights following Will's death. She felt herself returning back to normal, now that she was no longer medicated and her body had begun to heal. She was regaining clarity and decided it was time to start cooking again. Today was one of those rare days that Kate would be coming home early, and the two of them were looking forward to a dinner together.

Claire had planned a meal and although it was early, she had begun preparations. The first step was pouring herself a glass of wine which, as any chef would tell you, is a requirement of any successful meal. She left the glass half poured when she heard the doorbell, and she made her way to the front door. She was perplexed at the sight of Glen, the mechanic from Will's shop.

"I'm sorry to show up like this, but I wondered if we could talk for a minute." His voice was soft and although she didn't know him, his body language suggested some distress.

"Yes, of course, Glen. Please come in."

"If you don't mind, Claire, could you please come to sit in my car? I would feel more comfortable."

"Sure thing." She grabbed her coat and followed him outside. The wind had picked up, and the once-brilliant leaves had withered and fallen off the trees, all but for a few strays. Wrapping her coat around her tightly, she quickly headed towards Glen's car. She wasn't nervous but was definitely interested.

Following Glen, Claire realized that she had never taken a good look at him before. He was a small, frail man, quite unhealthy looking. He still wore his coveralls from the shop, and it looked like they had not been cleaned in some time. His pointed nose and thin chin added to his lizard-like features. As he opened the car door for her, she noticed that he had small hands and long, bony fingers. It was hard to tell if he hadn't washed his hands lately, or if the grease under his fingernails had become embedded over time. He walked around to the driver's side and shut his door with a loud bang. Once seated, and without hesitation, Glen looked at her with his anxious, beady eyes and said, "Will killed Elyse."

Chapter 39

"WHAT ARE YOU TELLING ME, GLEN?" CLAIRE PRACTICALLY shouted. "And why after all this time?"

"I wanted to tell you sooner, Claire. After the police had finished their investigation. I wanted to see if they uncovered anything on their own. Maybe I was hoping they could solve it."

"They wouldn't have had such a hard time if you had just told them, Glen."

He winced at this remark but continued.

"I couldn't come to see you in the hospital because I couldn't take the chance of being overheard. Then when you got home your mom was here, and I couldn't ever get you alone."

"Maybe you just should have let the secret die."

"I couldn't let it go. It's been eating me up. Ironically, Will only told me a few days before he died. Before that, I didn't believe that he was in any way connected to her death, let alone the one who killed her."

"What the hell happened then?" demanded Claire, becoming angry.

"Maria started calling Will about a year and a half after

she moved back home. She kept leaving messages for him. I was hoping that he wouldn't call her back, but eventually he did. I was so pissed. I mean, he had already gone through that with Elyse, why would he want to start up again with the other one?"

"So, it's true. He did start seeing her?"

"Yeah, not right away, but he did. She came to the shop one day, all dressed up in this tight little dress. She was a looker, there was no doubt. I guess Will found her irresistible. But after a year of it, I could see he was stressed. It had been a fling and it had run its course, but I think she wanted him to marry her or something."

"Well, what did he expect? She was still living at home and he was interested, so it's normal for her to want more from him."

"Yeah well, it wasn't a good situation. I kept trying to convince him to dump her. That's why I took him to the dance. I was hoping he'd meet someone new, to take his mind off her. And he did, Claire. He met you."

"Gee, thanks a lot, Glen," Claire hissed sarcastically. "What was I, the antidote for his disease?"

Glen looked over at her apologetically.

"Anyway, Will couldn't get rid of her after that, and he didn't know what to do. He was worried that Daniela might find out about it, like she did with Elyse. He told me that he was afraid that it would end up like the last time."

"What did that mean, like last time?"

"I guess he meant like when he was with Elyse, that last day when she died. Christ, the man knew better! I had told him to stay the hell away from her, and I believe Wolf told him same thing to him many times. Daniela was getting suspicious because he was spending less time with her and more time in the city, so she had Jack and Zack follow him to see what he was up to. She found out about the girl and hit the roof. Will tried to convince her that it was not as it seemed, that he was just friends with them through Jorge, but she warned him that he better end it, or the boys would be paying him a visit.

"Daniela again," snapped Claire.

"So, apparently on this day, he planned to tell Elyse that it was over," continued Glen. "I don't know exactly what happened, whether he did it on purpose, but next thing you know, she's dead. He said that she was stoned out of her mind. They fought, and she punched first. But he's a big guy, so I don't know how a punch from her could be threatening. I guess he hit back or something. He said that she was dead, just like that, and he panicked. I think he said that he drove around for an hour or so, with her sitting up, buckled into the passenger seat. He was waiting for it to get a bit darker so he could drive her out to the bluffs."

Claire was no longer shocked by this kind of news. No more stomach twists or laboured breaths. All she could feel now was anger and revulsion. That summer had been one very bizarre period in her life.

"So, was Will suggesting that he might have to do that again, with Maria?" Claire thought she would be sick and opened the car door for air. "Why didn't you go to the police, Glen?"

Even while she was asking this question, she knew why. For the same reason that she, Wolf, and even Maria had not gone to the police. Everyone was afraid, and none of them understood exactly who they should be afraid of. Such was the enigma surrounding Will and all those involved with him.

"I was scared that they would charge me with something! Withholding evidence or whatever. And I knew Will was afraid of Jack and Zack, and those guys know who I am, too. But mostly, I didn't come forward because I was still absorbing the shock that Will did it. He hadn't been back to the shop since he told me, and I was waiting to talk to him. He didn't explain it very well, and he was jabbering and ranting, so I needed him to tell me just how Elyse died again. I never had the chance to ask a second time. He was dead, and I felt fucked up all over again. All of this is like it's not even real."

"And I guess once he was dead, it made no difference, is that what you thought, Glen?" asked Claire.

"Well, yeah, that's exactly it. Nobody could prove anything at this point. Elyse has been dead a long time by now, and then Will dies, see? So, who needs to know! Except for you. I thought you deserved to know."

"Deserved? I *deserved* to know? How did you come to the rationalization? What does that even mean?"

"Because I think you cared a lot for him, and I don't want you to care for him any longer. And I know that you wanted to know what really happened to Elyse," said Glen awkwardly. "But I think we should just bury this with him."

Claire looked at him with a mixture of confusion and loathing. "I didn't care for him, Glen. I certainly didn't care for him in the way that you are suggesting. I liked him, that's all. And I haven't even liked him since his memorial service and my conversation with Bonnie."

"Look Claire, do with this what you want. I could go to the police, or you could. I couldn't say anything until I knew that Jack and Zack were out of the picture. Those two knew the police would have nothing on them, and they would have known that I was the one who spoke up. I didn't want to end up face down in a pond somewhere. But I needed to tell someone, or else it would have driven me crazy. This is like my confession or something."

Glen calmed down a little as he continued, "But what can be done now? They are both dead, the case is closed. The search for answers is over, and the search for Maria's killer is over. Now they are searching for Jack, whom they may never find. I think I would just prefer to let this go. We can leave it between you and me, okay, Claire? Do you really want to stir this up all over again?"

Without a word, Claire briefly gave him a look of surrender and left the car. The slam of the door affirmed their understanding. She tried to hold back the tears until she reached the house. The dry, dead leaves swirled around her feet as she opened her front door and disappeared inside.

After Glen had driven away, Claire rushed to her dark room and began a frantic search through some boxes on the shelf. Shortly after Will's death, she had been developing some film from an earlier shoot and had come across a photo of him at his cottage. Back then, she had just glanced at it and stuck it in this box, forgetting about it until now. It was the day they were idly sitting by the pond. She had taken out her camera while Will was seated a distance away, throwing pebbles into the water.

When she had developed the pictures, she noticed the expression on Will's face but had assumed he was lost in thought, unaware that he was being photographed. Finding it at last, she brought it into the light and examined it again. Will looked tormented, almost evil. He had a blank look on his face, but there was something in his eyes. What she was looking at was akin to madness or hysteria. It was all very subtle, but she saw it. And she recalled his body language. He wasn't just tossing the pebbles—he was plunging them into the water with a fury.

At the time, she had thought nothing of it, perhaps frustrated over something that happened at work. But now she was not so sure. She remembered the day that Cooper and Smitty had questioned her about Will acting strangely. Yes, she had answered. He had a bad dream on her last evening there. But it had been a bit more than that. She was asleep beside him and he had woken up with a bloodcurdling cry, his entire body covered in perspiration.

"Just a nightmare," he had told her. "I dreamt that a car fell on me in the shop." As he was closing his eyes, he had mumbled, "Claire, do you believe we get what we deserve?" Then he had fallen back to sleep.

"Just a dream," she had said to herself as she too closed her eyes.

She had left very early the following morning. It was still dark, and Will was sound asleep. It was the last time she ever saw him. But then, he had called her and instantly hung up. Was he planning on confessing? Did he have a change of heart? Did he plan on ending their relationship as well? Or was it because he heard a car coming? Like Glen, even if she had questions, they would remain unasked and unanswered.

Claire looked at the photo one last time before tearing it into little pieces and returned to the kitchen. Her wine was waiting.

"Let go of it," she heard her grandmother tell her. *Otpustit' eto, Clara.*

"So, what time is your flight?" asked Kate.

"Ben thinks we should be there by seven, but I'm finding it hard to think about going."

"I hope you are joking, Claire."

"Yes, I think I am, but it's hard leaving after all that's happened. I can't describe how the past months have changed me. I think I've had enough adventure to last me a lifetime, and I certainly won't be searching for any."

Trying for nonchalance, she added, "I do have something big on my mind, but it can wait until I get back. I can think about it while I'm gone."

But then, with a sudden turn, she said to Kate, "But maybe I don't have to wait until I get back. Sorry Kate, I forgot to do something." She ran up the stairs to her room and closed the door. Finding the business card that Smitty had given her, she picked up the phone and dialed the number. With determination she waited on hold, anxious to speak with the policeman. This thing needed to stop. She had been silent long enough.

"Hello, Officer Smitty? Hi, it's Claire Perova. I have something I think you'll want to hear."

Her next call would be to her friend Wolf, and then she would feel free to leave.

"I will miss you Claire. Please hug Paul for me, and take lots of pictures. I'm sure you remember how to use that camera of yours? Oh, and please stay away from ponds and red-headed men!"

Kate looked so beautiful and innocent. She would miss her friend.

With that, the two friends hugged tightly as Ben's car pulled into the driveway. An excited Adam ran over to grab Claire's suitcases.

Claire, Ben, and Adam were now settled into their seats on the British Airways Jumbo 747, headed for Manchester, England, where Paul and Suki and their son Nigel would be waiting to drive them to Bakewell. Claire was looking forward to walking along the River Wye with her little brother. An announcement from the pilot informed them that their departure from the gate had been delayed by fifteen minutes, so Claire reached into her bag to take out the last letter from Paul, which included their instructions of where to meet them.

Ben smiled at Adam, who was nestled safely between the two of them.

"Read me that part again, the one about the food," he whispered to Claire over Adam's head.

"Okay, here it is." She opened Paul's crumpled, oft-read letter. She read: "I just want to warn you that the British cuisine is in dire need of repair. However, all is not lost, as Suki's curry dishes are the best in the world, particularly her Rogan Josh. I know you will love the flavours, and she's looking forward to cooking with you. And hey, I have a good friend, Robert, who lives in the Hunters Bar region of Sheffield. He knows all the best Indian restaurants in Sheffield, and he has insisted that we pay him a visit."

Ben laughed again before settling in for the flight. "Sounds better every time I hear it!"

Adam smiled up at Claire before opening his new coloring book, something she had bought for the holiday. As the plane slowly began to lurch backward from the gate, Claire closed her eyes and leaned into the headrest. As she did so, she felt peacefulness overcome her. She had not felt this way for many years. She felt the presence of Oliver and her grandparents snuggled up next to her, holding her hands, drawing her closer to them. She smiled. Her next challenge would obviously be the Rogan Josh.

It is our history that characterizes who we are. Our struggles will strengthen us, our experiences define us, and the future lies ahead. It's ours to create. Our memories and secrets are buried deep inside of us, some deeper than others.

In a rousing grand finale, Clara Perova's musical genius extrordinaire played Nina Simone's "Feeling Good" as the plane left the ground.

I DON'T HAVE THE RIGHT WORDS TO THANK FRANK GIAMPA, for his enthusiastic support, his interest in this book and his strong desire that it get done right. Your friendship means a great deal to me.

To my husband David, who has patiently endured my disappearing for hours at a time to write. Thank you for keeping me laughing.

And to my daughter Jennifer, who offered moral support and good advice along with her excellent proof reading. You are my shining light whom I admire more and more with each passing day.

Cover photo by Oliver Koh at Upsplash.

Author's Note

THANK YOU SO MUCH FOR READING MY FIRST BOOK. WHILE it is a work of fiction, it contains certain elements that are a big part of me and of my life. This was a great way for me to make those parts come alive through my story telling.

I appreciate all reviews, good or bad. No writer can continue to write if there are no readers. Your feedback is what will sustain my writing and keep me working. Please accept my gratitude at how much your feedback means to me personally. I thank you with the utmost sincerity.

Please go to your favourite website, be it Friesen's, Goodreads, Bookish, Amazon or any others, and submit your review.

www.alyhallwriter.com

About the Author

ALYSSA HALL WRITES FROM the heart. Like the protagonist of *Trusting Claire*, Alyssa grew up in Ontario in a family of Russian immigrants. Claire's Grecian adventures, culinary appreciation, and small-town background all stem from Alyssa's real life. Most importantly, Claire and her creator both approach life with curiosity, tenacity, and grit.

Alyssa wrote this, her debut novel for those who, like her, enjoy a good psychological murder mystery. At the same time, she wrote *Trusting Claire* with an attention to the more subtle aspects of everyday life: the experiences of immigrant families in Canada. She touches on the nuances of mother-daughter relationships and also the difficult work of interpreting what our hearts tell us.

Alyssa now lives in Langley, British Columbia, with her husband, David. She is the proud mother of her daughter, Jennifer and her two stepdaughters, Natalie and Shelly.